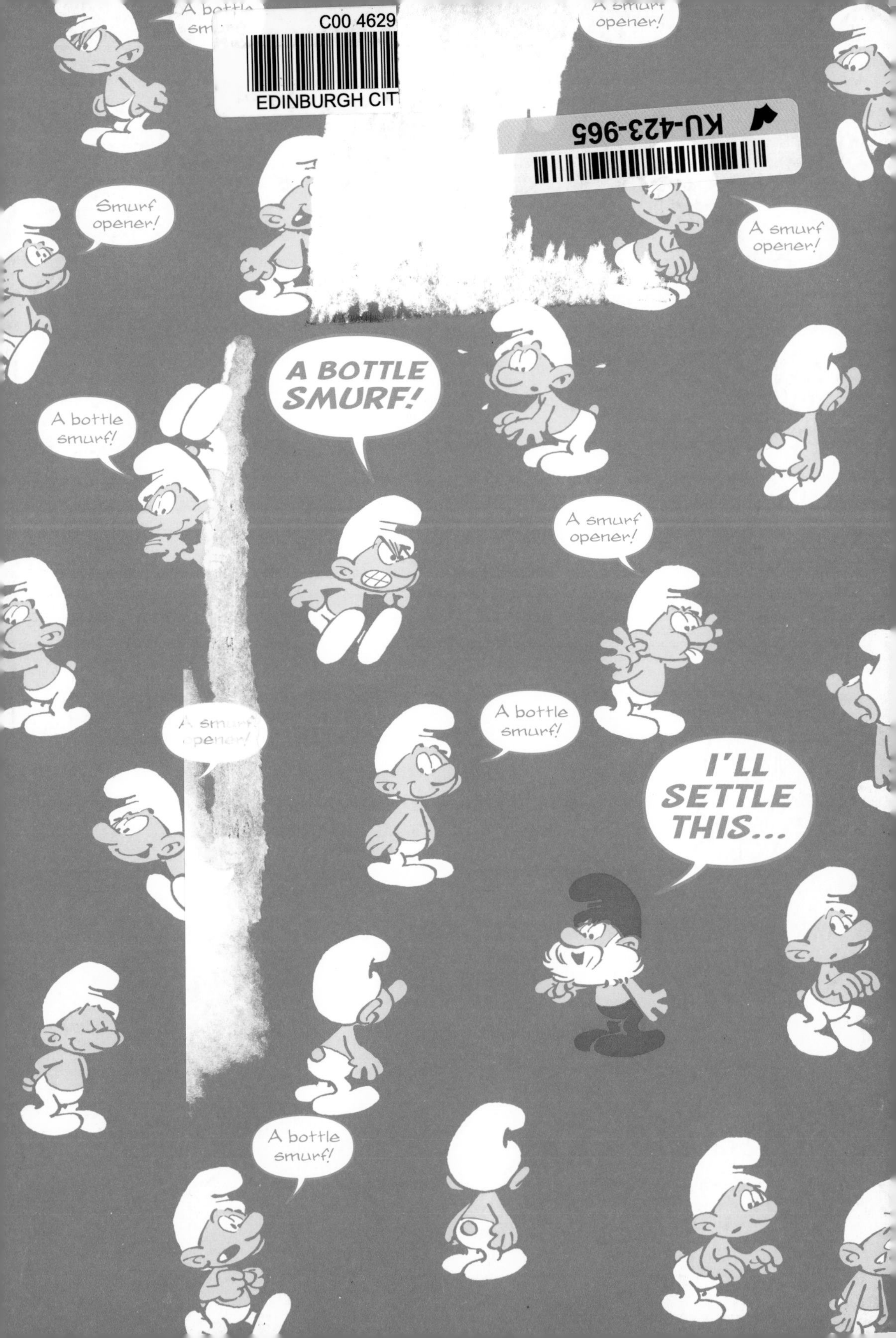
Smurf opener!
A smurf opener!
A BOTTLE SMURF!
A bottle smurf!
A smurf opener!
A smurf opener!
A bottle smurf!
I'LL SETTLE THIS...
A bottle smurf!

# SMURF VS. SMURF

Peyo

DOWN WITH NORTHERNERS
THE SOUTH SAYS SMURF TO YOU

DOWN WITH SOUTHERNERS!
OVERCOME

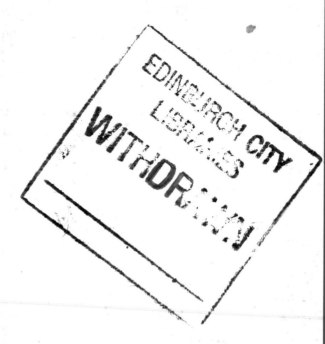

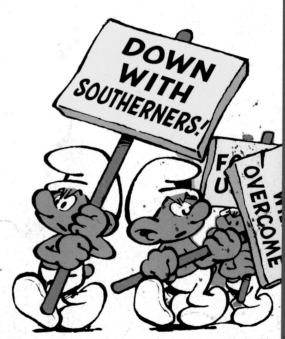

# SMURF VS. SMURF

NO
THE SOUTH WILL OVERCOME.
SMURF-OPENER AND NOT BOTTLE-SMURF!
SMURF FOR THE SOUTH
VIVA THE NORTH
DOWN WITH NORTHERNERS
14

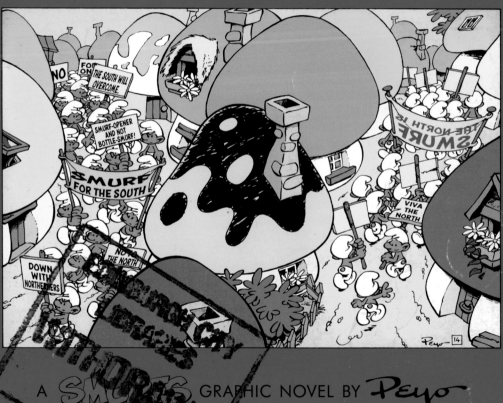

A SMURFS GRAPHIC NOVEL BY PEYO
AND
YVAN DELPORTE

OR BY
YVAN DELPORTE AND PEYO

PAPERCUTZ™
NEW YORK

## SMURFS GRAPHIC NOVELS AVAILABLE FROM PAPERCUTZ™

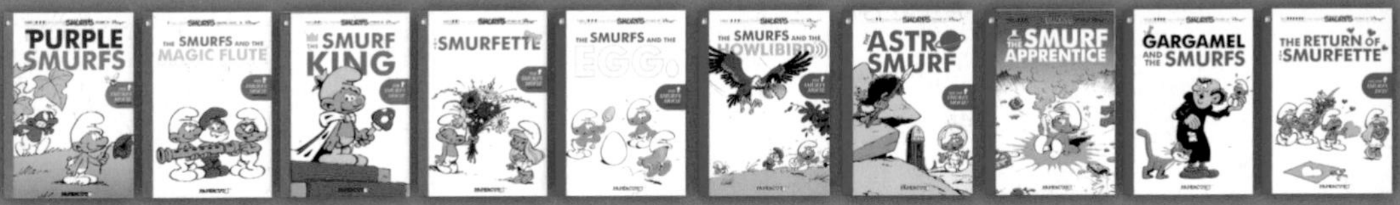
PURPLE SMURFS
THE SMURFS AND THE MAGIC FLUTE
THE SMURF KING
SMURFETTE
THE SMURFS AND THE EGG
THE SMURFS AND THE HOWLIBIRD
ASTRO SMURF
THE SMURF APPRENTICE
GARGAMEL AND THE SMURFS
THE RETURN OF THE SMURFETTE

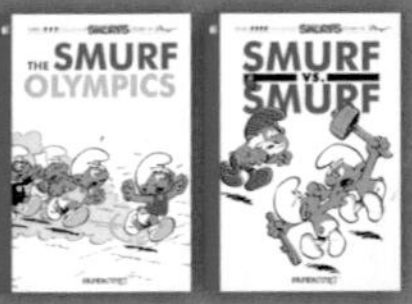
THE SMURF OLYMPICS
SMURF VS. SMURF

1. **THE PURPLE SMURFS**
2. **THE SMURFS AND THE MAGIC FLUTE**
3. **THE SMURF KING**
4. **THE SMURFETTE**
5. **THE SMURFS AND THE EGG**
6. **THE SMURFS AND THE HOWLIBIRD**
7. **THE ASTROSMURF**
8. **THE SMURF APPRENTICE**
9. **GARGAMEL AND THE SMURFS**
10. **THE RETURN OF THE SMURFETTE**
11. **THE SMURF OLYMPICS**
12. **SMURF VS. SMURF**

**COMING SOON:**

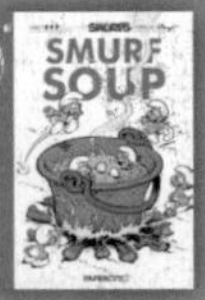
SMURF SOUP

13. **SMURF SOUP**

THE SMURFS graphic novels are available in paperback for $5.99 each and in hardcover for $10.99 each at booksellers everywhere. Or order from us. Please add $4.00 for postage and handling for the first book, add $1.00 for each additional book. Please make check payable to NBM Publishing. Send to: PAPERCUTZ, 160 Broadway, Suite 700, East Wing New York, NY 10038 (1-800-886-1223)

THE SMURFS graphic novels are also available digitally from COMIXOLOGY.com.

*WWW.PAPERCUTZ.COM*

## SMURF VS. SMURF



"Smurf Vs. Smurf"
*BY YVAN DELPORTE AND PEYO*

"The Painter Smurf"
*BY PEYO*

"The Smurf Vacation"
*BY PEYO*

"Easter Smurfs"
*BY PEYO*

Joe Johnson, *SMURFLATIONS*
Adam Grano, *SMURFIC DESIGN*
Janice Chiang, *LETTERING SMURFETTE*
Matt. Murray, *SMURF CONSULTANT*
Michael Petranek, *ASSOCIATE SMURF*
Jim Salicrup, *SMURF-IN-CHIEF*

*PAPERBACK EDITION ISBN: 978-1-59707-320-2*
*HARDCOVER EDITION ISBN: 978-1-59707-321-9*

*PRINTED IN CHINA JUNE 2012 BY WKT CO. LTD.*
*3/F PHASE I LEADER INDUSTRIAL CENTRE*
*188 TEXACO ROAD, TSEUN WAN, N.T., HONG KONG*

*DISTRIBUTED BY MACMILLAN*
*FIRST PAPERCUTZ PRINTING*

# SMURF VERSUS SMURF

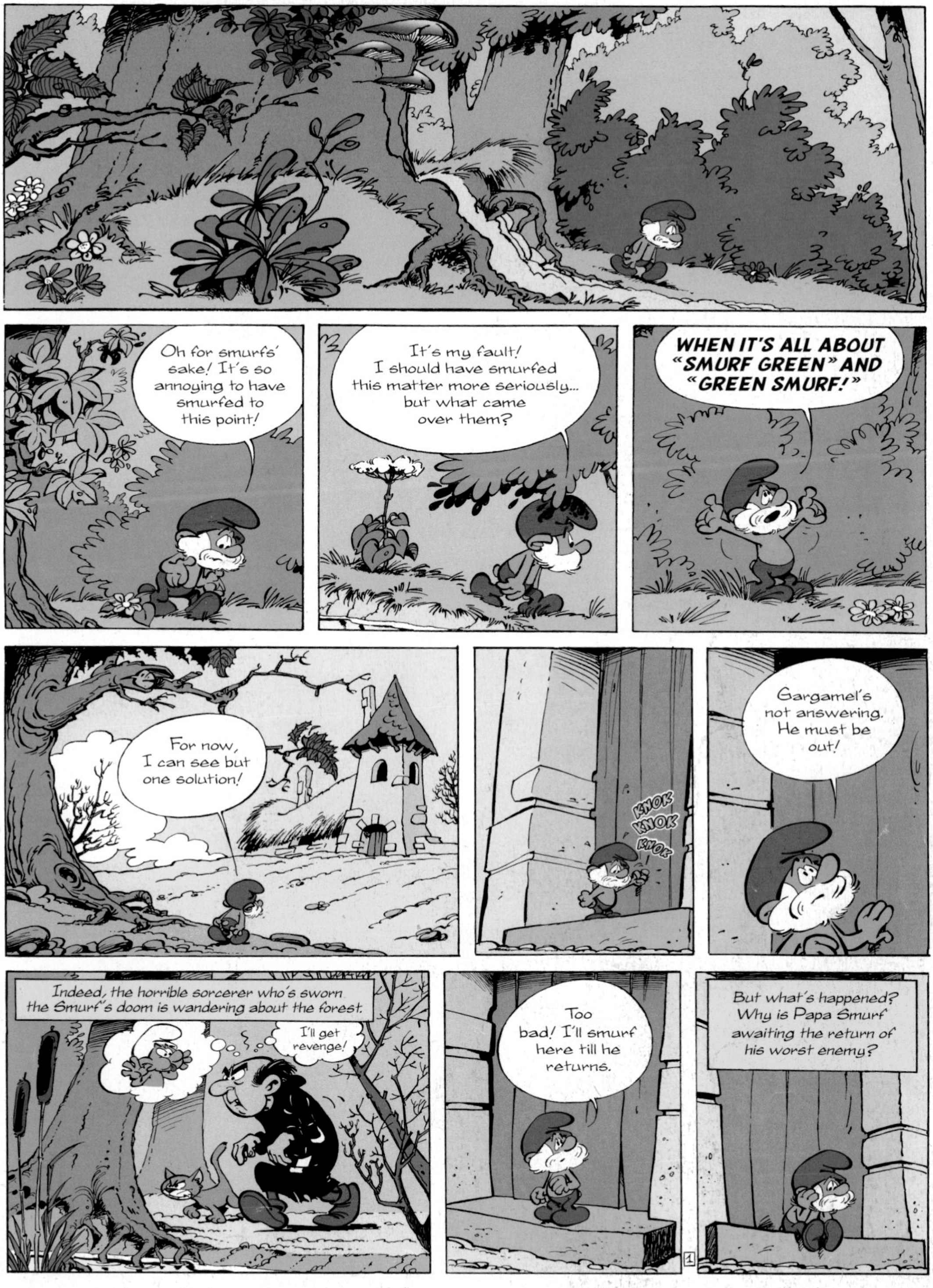
Oh for smurfs' sake! It's so annoying to have smurfed to this point!
It's my fault! I should have smurfed this matter more seriously... but what came over them?
WHEN IT'S ALL ABOUT "SMURF GREEN" AND "GREEN SMURF!"
For now, I can see but one solution!
KNOK KNOK KNOK
Gargamel's not answering. He must be out!
Indeed, the horrible sorcerer who's sworn the Smurf's doom is wandering about the forest.
I'll get revenge!
Too bad! I'll smurf here till he returns.
1
But what's happened? Why is Papa Smurf awaiting the return of his worst enemy?

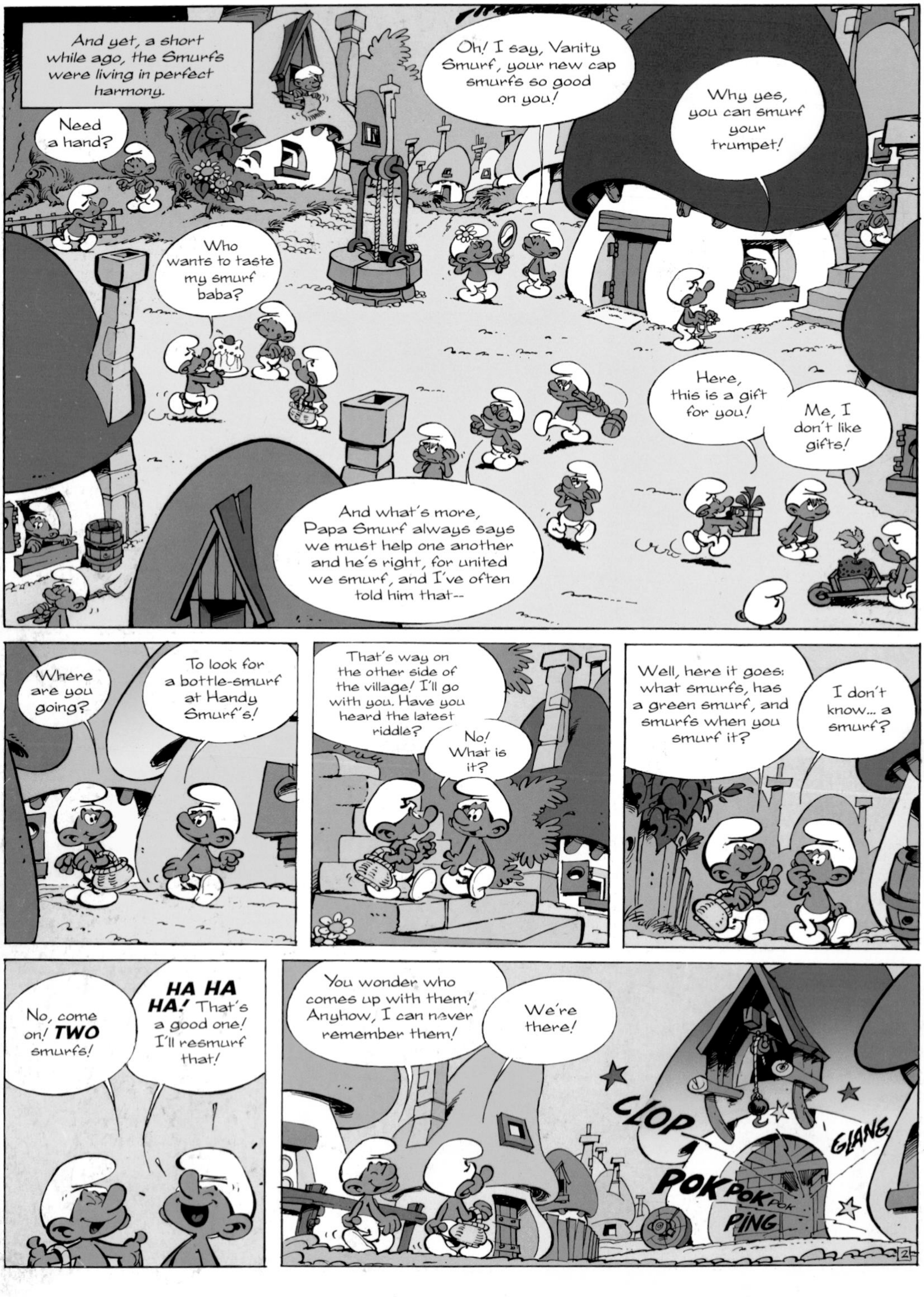

And yet, a short while ago, the Smurfs were living in perfect harmony.
Need a hand?
Oh! I say, Vanity Smurf, your new cap smurfs so good on you!
Why yes, you can smurf your trumpet!
Who wants to taste my smurf baba?
Here, this is a gift for you!
Me, I don't like gifts!
And what's more, Papa Smurf always says we must help one another and he's right, for united we smurf, and I've often told him that--
Where are you going?
To look for a bottle-smurf at Handy Smurf's!
That's way on the other side of the village! I'll go with you. Have you heard the latest riddle?
No! What is it?
Well, here it goes: what smurfs, has a green smurf, and smurfs when you smurf it?
I don't know... a smurf?
No, come on! TWO smurfs!
HA HA HA! That's a good one! I'll resmurf that!
You wonder who comes up with them! Anyhow, I can never remember them!
We're there!
CLOP
GLANG
POK POK POK
PING
2

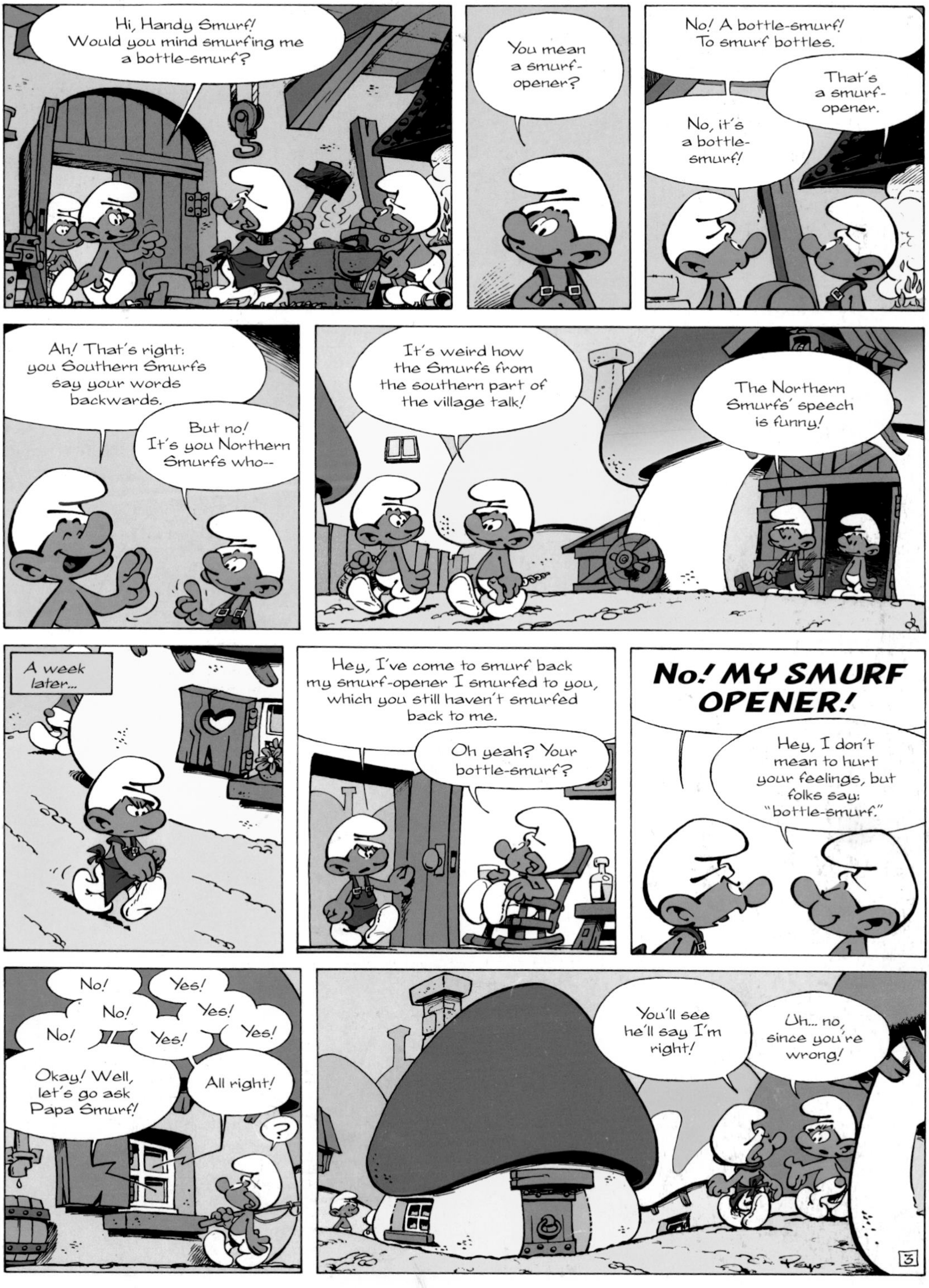
Hi, Handy Smurf! Would you mind smurfing me a bottle-smurf?
You mean a smurf-opener?
No! A bottle-smurf! To smurf bottles.
No, it's a bottle-smurf!
That's a smurf-opener.
Ah! That's right: you Southern Smurfs say your words backwards.
But no! It's you Northern Smurfs who--
It's weird how the Smurfs from the southern part of the village talk!
The Northern Smurfs' speech is funny!
A week later...
Hey, I've come to smurf back my smurf-opener I smurfed to you, which you still haven't smurfed back to me.
Oh yeah? Your bottle-smurf?
No! MY SMURF OPENER!
Hey, I don't mean to hurt your feelings, but folks say: "bottle-smurf."
No!
Yes!
No!
Yes!
No!
Yes!
Yes!
Okay! Well, let's go ask Papa Smurf!
All right!
?
You'll see he'll say I'm right!
Uh... no, since you're wrong!
3

And a pinch of lycopodium, which I smurf into the--

NOK NOK NOK

What's that?

Papa Smurf, he claims you have to say bottle-smurf even though everyone knows full well--

Papa Smurf, isn't it wrong to say smurf-opener instead of--

Listen, my little Smurfs, right now I'm smurfing a *VERY, VERY* important experiment! So, for this tiny dispute, could you come resmurf me about it some other time?

A smurf-opener!

No! A bottle-smurf!

What's wrong? What's wrong?

Poet Smurf, you're from the South, I'll smurf you as a witness. Do we say bottle-smurf or smurf-opener?

A bottle-smurf, no?

Well, yes!

Ah, no!

Wait, I'll go smurf my grammar smurf!

You Smurfs from up North always put the word smurf afterwards! But you should say: "smurfapples" and not "pinesmurfs," because otherwise you could confuse it with "smurf-cones"!

Well...

But then you'd confuse "smurf-cones" with "ice cream smurfs"!

And "pine-smurfs" with "smurf slices"!

So here! I'll get you all to agree. It smurfs here that any past participle used with "to smurf" takes an *ED* in the past tense, if the word ends in--

?

I'd say: "Smurfs smurf"!

But no, *ON THE CONTRARY!*

You Smurfs from down South, you smurf backwards!

Ah, no! That's you all!

Me, I don't like bottle-openers!

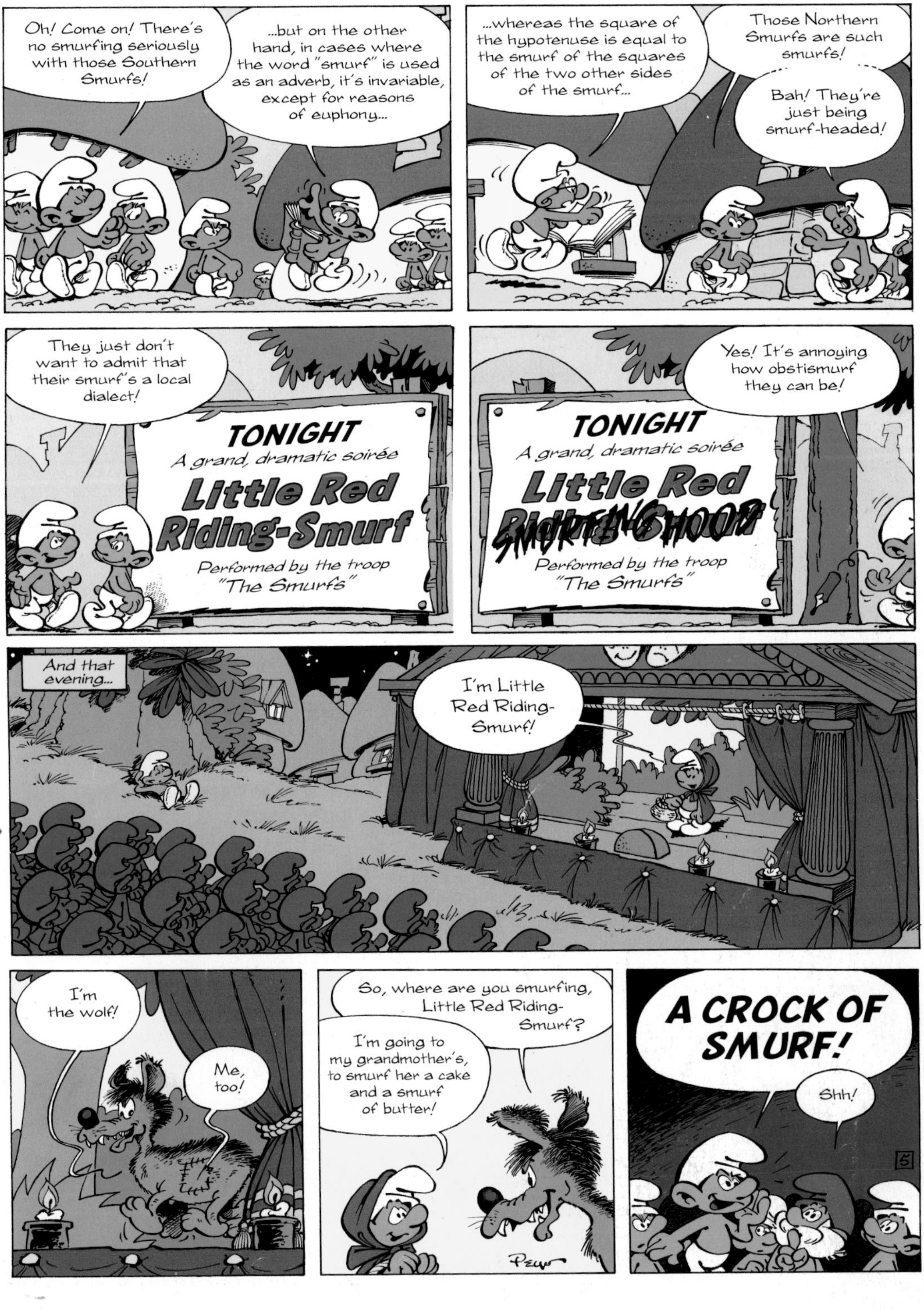

Oh! Come on! There's no smurfing seriously with those Southern Smurfs!
...but on the other hand, in cases where the word "smurf" is used as an adverb, it's invariable, except for reasons of euphony...
...whereas the square of the hypotenuse is equal to the smurf of the squares of the two other sides of the smurf...
Those Northern Smurfs are such smurfs!
Bah! They're just being smurf-headed!
They just don't want to admit that their smurf's a local dialect!
TONIGHT
A grand, dramatic soirée
Little Red Riding-Smurf
Performed by the troop "The Smurfs"
Yes! It's annoying how obstismurf they can be!
TONIGHT
A grand, dramatic soirée
Little Red
Performed by the troop "The Smurfs"
And that evening...
I'm Little Red Riding-Smurf!
I'm the wolf!
Me, too!
So, where are you smurfing, Little Red Riding-Smurf?
I'm going to my grandmother's, to smurf her a cake and a smurf of butter!
A CROCK OF SMURF!
Shh!
5

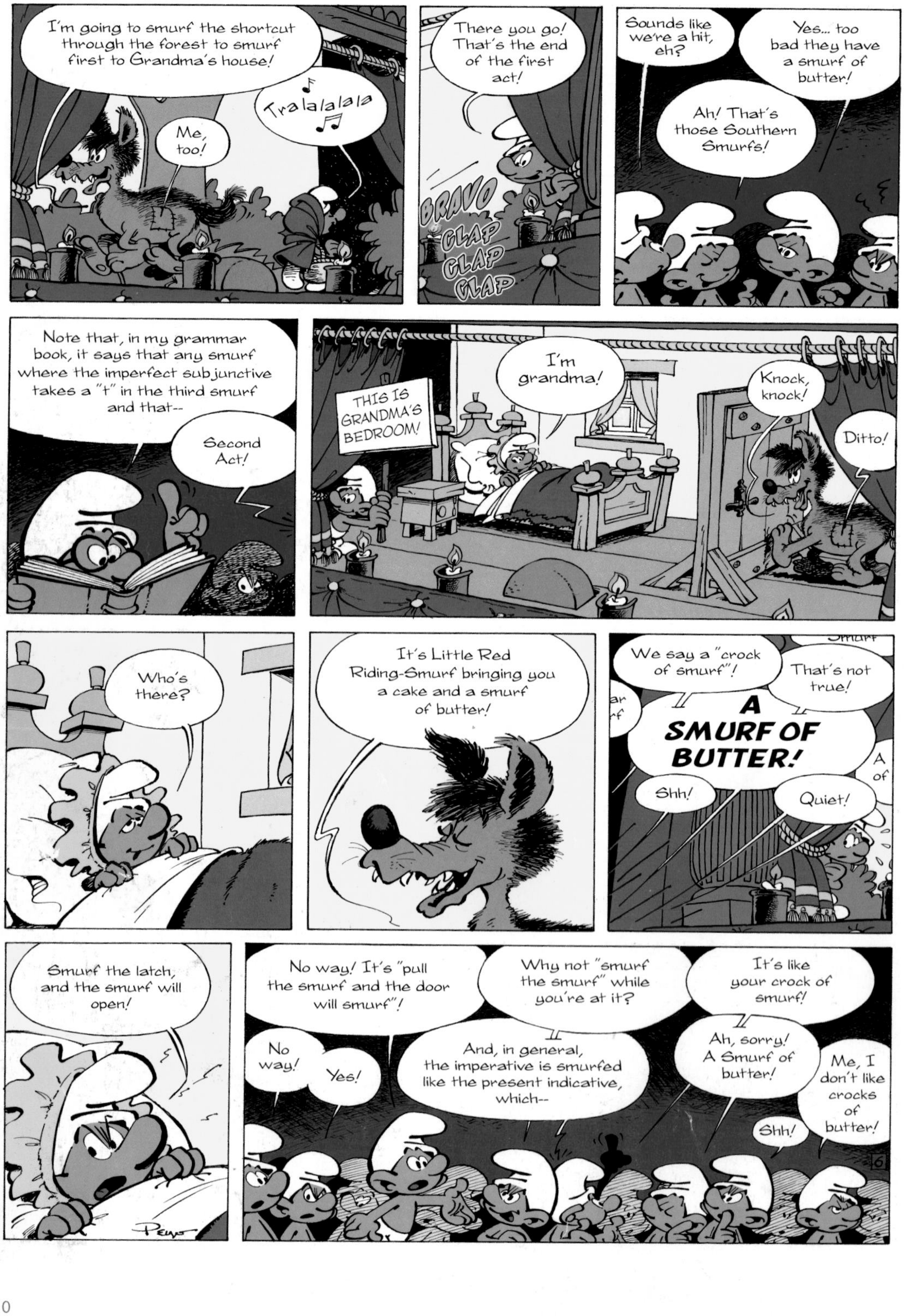
I'm going to smurf the shortcut through the forest to smurf first to Grandma's house!
Me, too!
Tralalalala
There you go! That's the end of the first act!
BRAVO
CLAP
CLAP
CLAP
Sounds like we're a hit, eh?
Yes... too bad they have a smurf of butter!
Ah! That's those Southern Smurfs!
Note that, in my grammar book, it says that any smurf where the imperfect subjunctive takes a "t" in the third smurf and that--
Second Act!
THIS IS GRANDMA'S BEDROOM!
I'm grandma!
Knock, knock!
Ditto!
Who's there?
It's Little Red Riding-Smurf bringing you a cake and a smurf of butter!
We say a "crock of smurf"!
That's not true!
A SMURF OF BUTTER!
Shh!
Quiet!
Smurf the latch, and the smurf will open!
PEYO
No way! It's "pull the smurf and the door will smurf"!
Why not "smurf the smurf" while you're at it?
It's like your crock of smurf!
No way!
Yes!
And, in general, the imperative is smurfed like the present indicative, which--
Ah, sorry! A Smurf of butter!
Me, I don't like crocks of butter!
Shh!
6

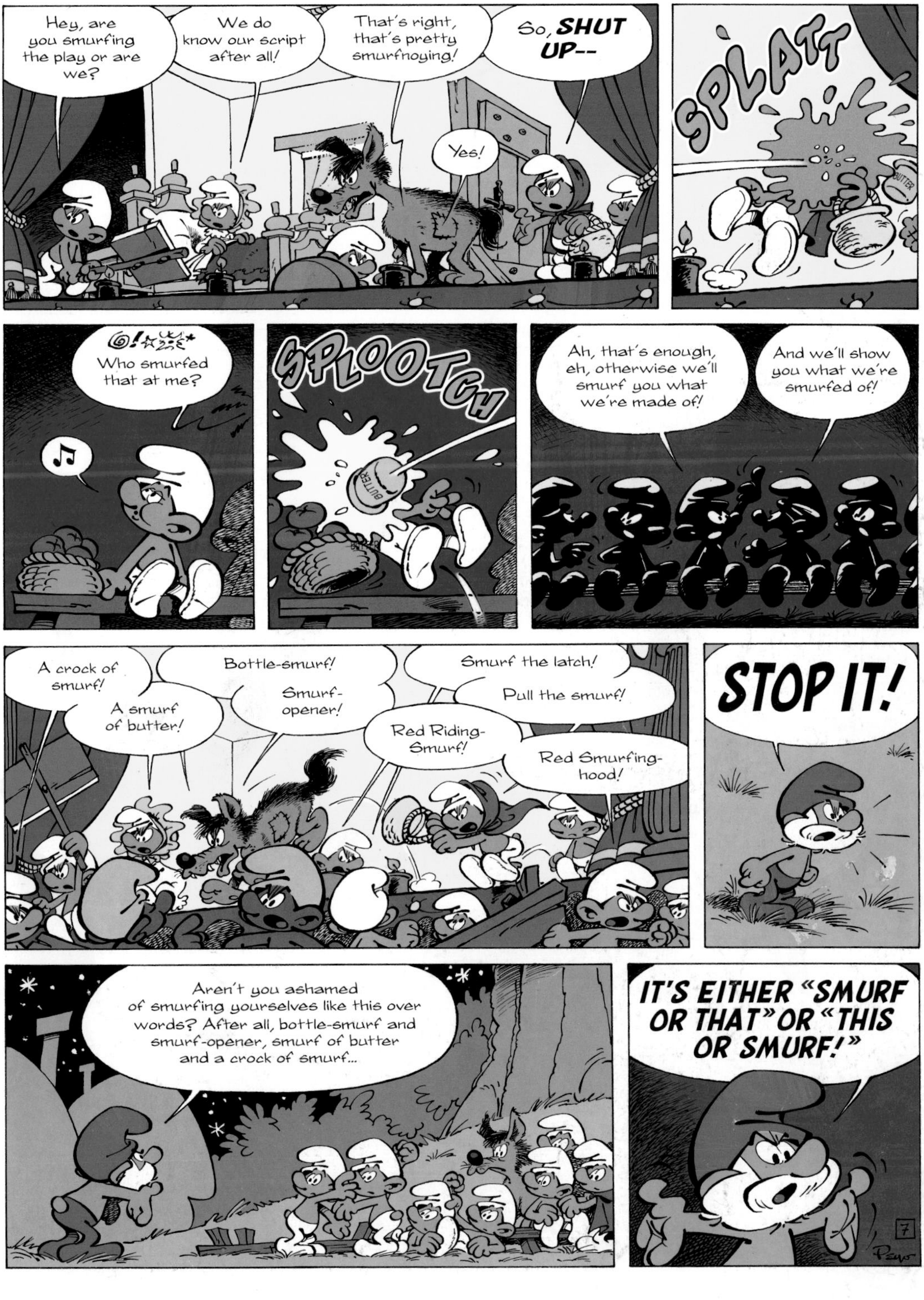
Hey, are you smurfing the play or are we?
We do know our script after all!
That's right, that's pretty smurfnoying!
Yes!
So, SHUT UP--
SPLATT
BUTTER
Who smurfed that at me?
SPLOOTCH
BUTTER
Ah, that's enough, eh, otherwise we'll smurf you what we're made of!
And we'll show you what we're smurfed of!
A crock of smurf!
A smurf of butter!
Bottle-smurf!
Smurf-opener!
Smurf the latch!
Pull the smurf!
Red Riding-Smurf!
Red Smurfing-hood!
STOP IT!
Aren't you ashamed of smurfing yourselves like this over words? After all, bottle-smurf and smurf-opener, smurf of butter and a crock of smurf...
IT'S EITHER "SMURF OR THAT" OR "THIS OR SMURF!"
7

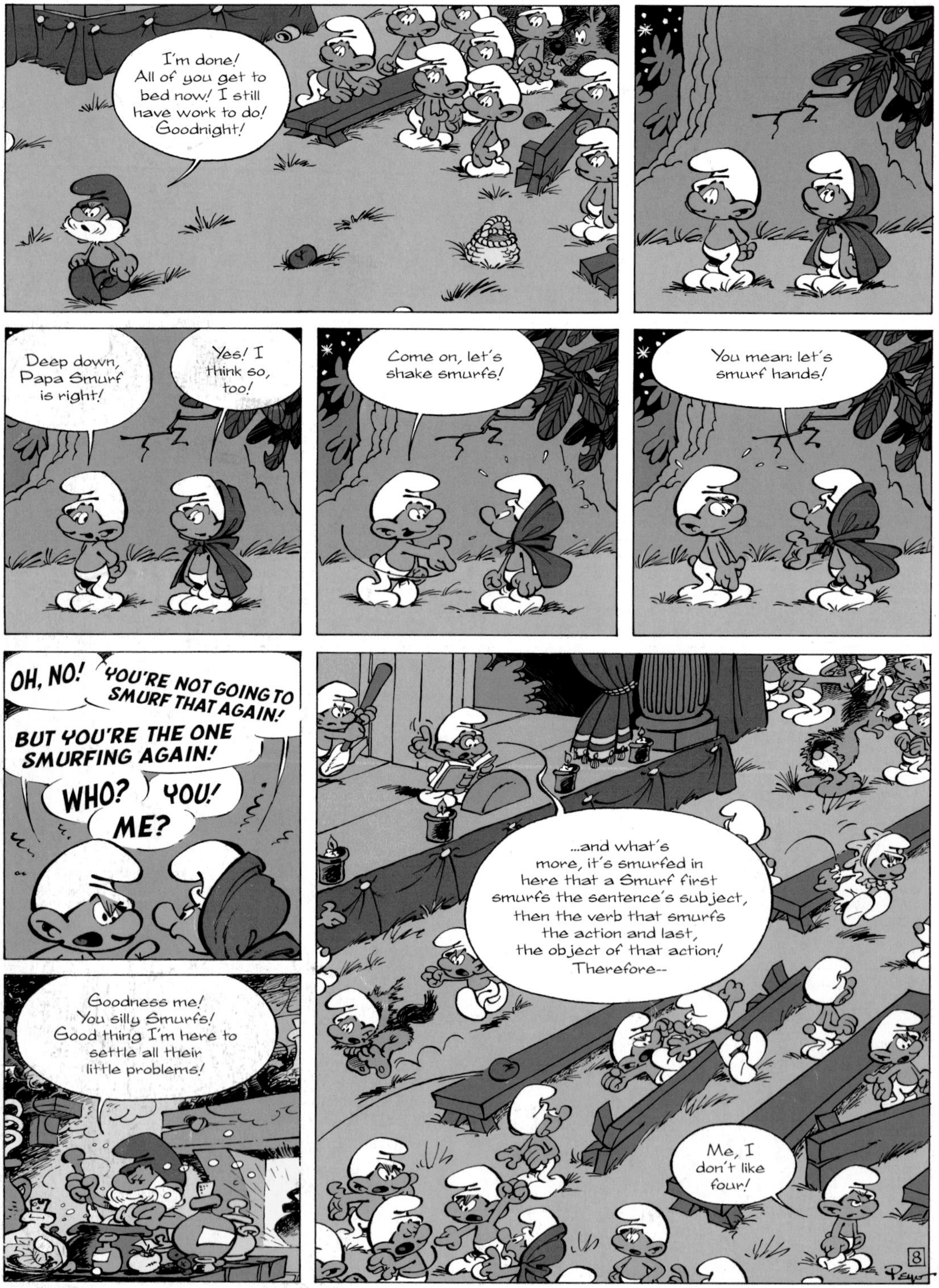

I'm done! All of you get to bed now! I still have work to do! Goodnight!
Deep down, Papa Smurf is right!
Yes! I think so, too!
Come on, let's shake smurfs!
You mean: let's smurf hands!
OH, NO!
YOU'RE NOT GOING TO SMURF THAT AGAIN!
BUT YOU'RE THE ONE SMURFING AGAIN!
WHO?
YOU!
ME?
...and what's more, it's smurfed in here that a Smurf first smurfs the sentence's subject, then the verb that smurfs the action and last, the object of that action! Therefore--
Me, I don't like four!
Goodness me! You silly Smurfs! Good thing I'm here to settle all their little problems!
8

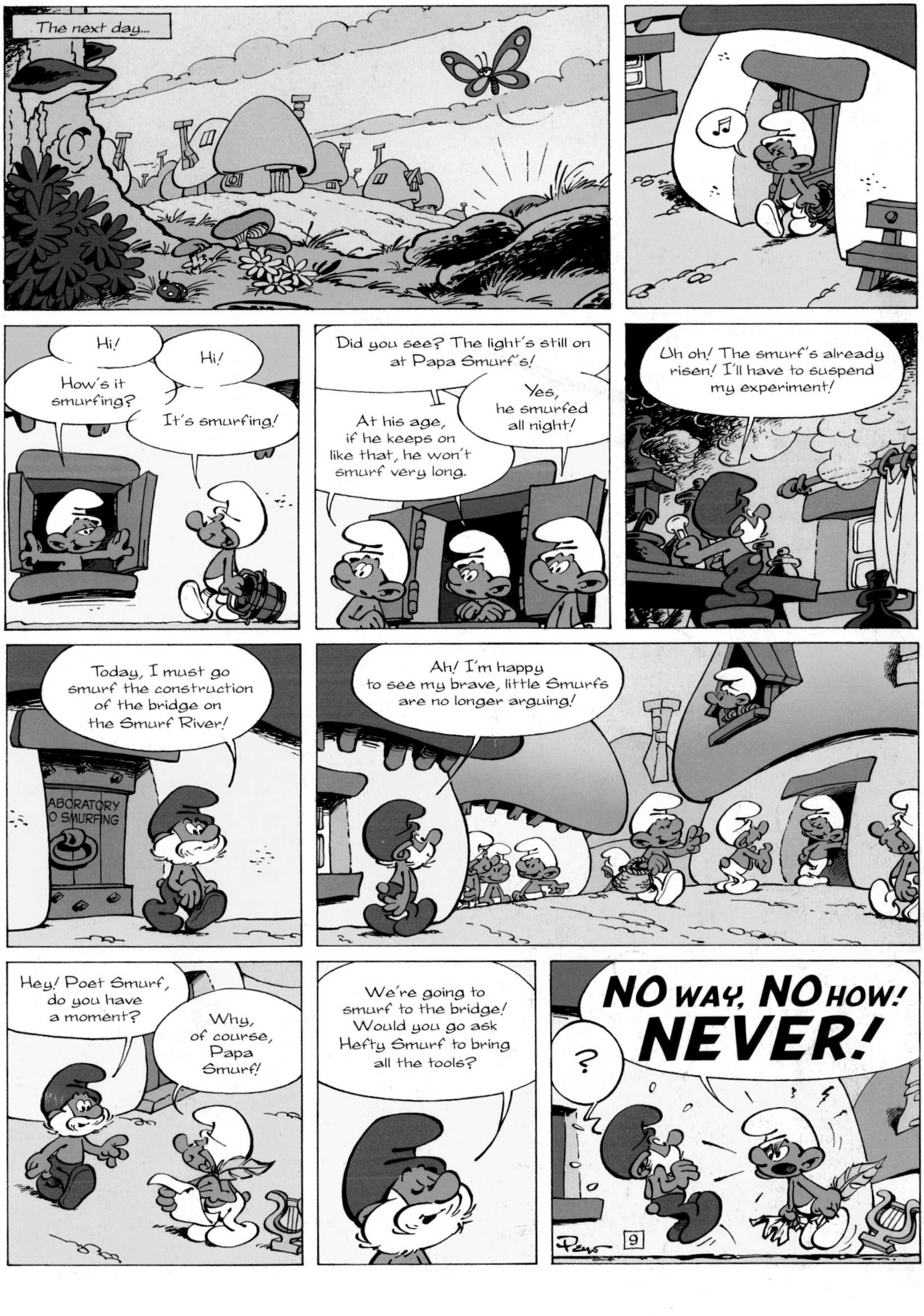
The next day...
Hi!
Hi!
How's it smurfing?
It's smurfing!
Did you see? The light's still on at Papa Smurf's!
Yes, he smurfed all night!
At his age, if he keeps on like that, he won't smurf very long.
Uh oh! The smurf's already risen! I'll have to suspend my experiment!
Today, I must go smurf the construction of the bridge on the Smurf River!
ABORATORY
O SMURFING
Ah! I'm happy to see my brave, little Smurfs are no longer arguing!
Hey! Poet Smurf, do you have a moment?
Why, of course, Papa Smurf!
We're going to smurf to the bridge! Would you go ask Hefty Smurf to bring all the tools?
?
NO WAY, NO HOW! NEVER!
9

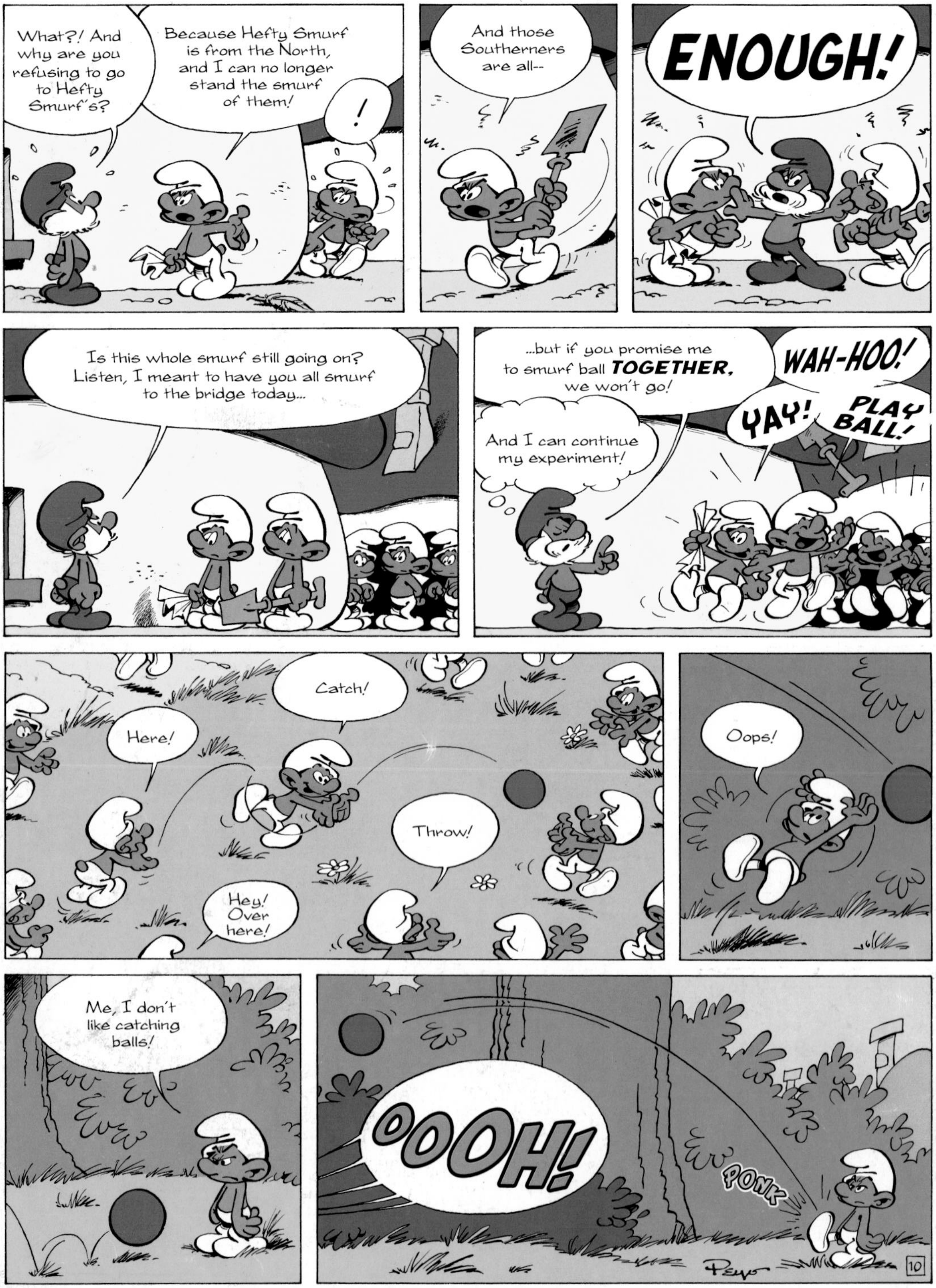
What?! And why are you refusing to go to Hefty Smurf's?
Because Hefty Smurf is from the North, and I can no longer stand the smurf of them!
!
And those Southerners are all--
ENOUGH!
Is this whole smurf still going on? Listen, I meant to have you all smurf to the bridge today...
...but if you promise me to smurf ball TOGETHER, we won't go!
And I can continue my experiment!
WAH-HOO!
YAY!
PLAY BALL!
Catch!
Here!
Throw!
Hey! Over here!
Oops!
Me, I don't like catching balls!
OOOH!
PONK
10

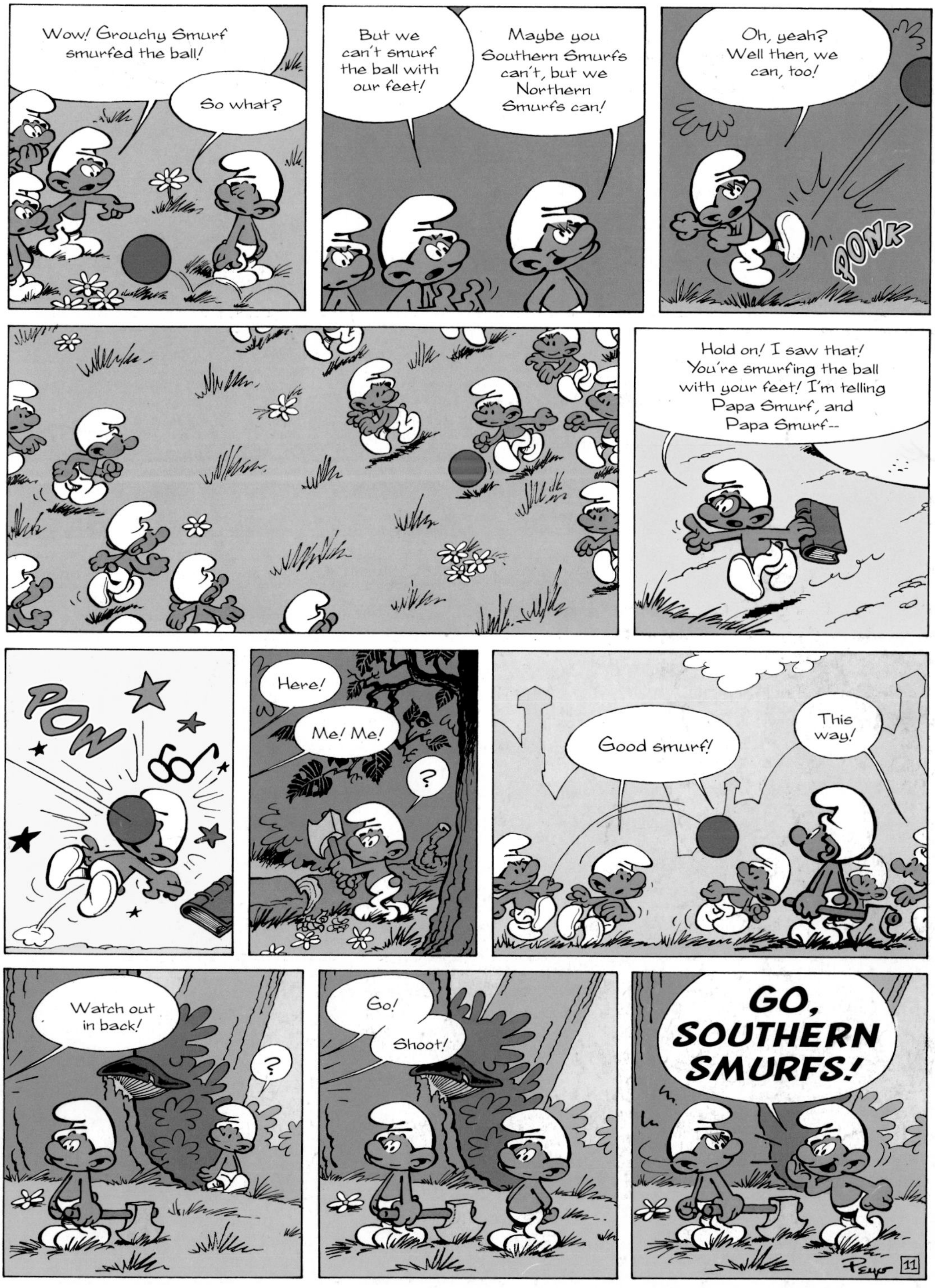
Wow! Grouchy Smurf smurfed the ball!
So what?
But we can't smurf the ball with our feet!
Maybe you Southern Smurfs can't, but we Northern Smurfs can!
Oh, yeah? Well then, we can, too!
PONK
Hold on! I saw that! You're smurfing the ball with your feet! I'm telling Papa Smurf, and Papa Smurf--
POW
Here!
Me! Me!
?
Good smurf!
This way!
Watch out in back!
?
Go!
Shoot!
GO, SOUTHERN SMURFS!
Peyo
11

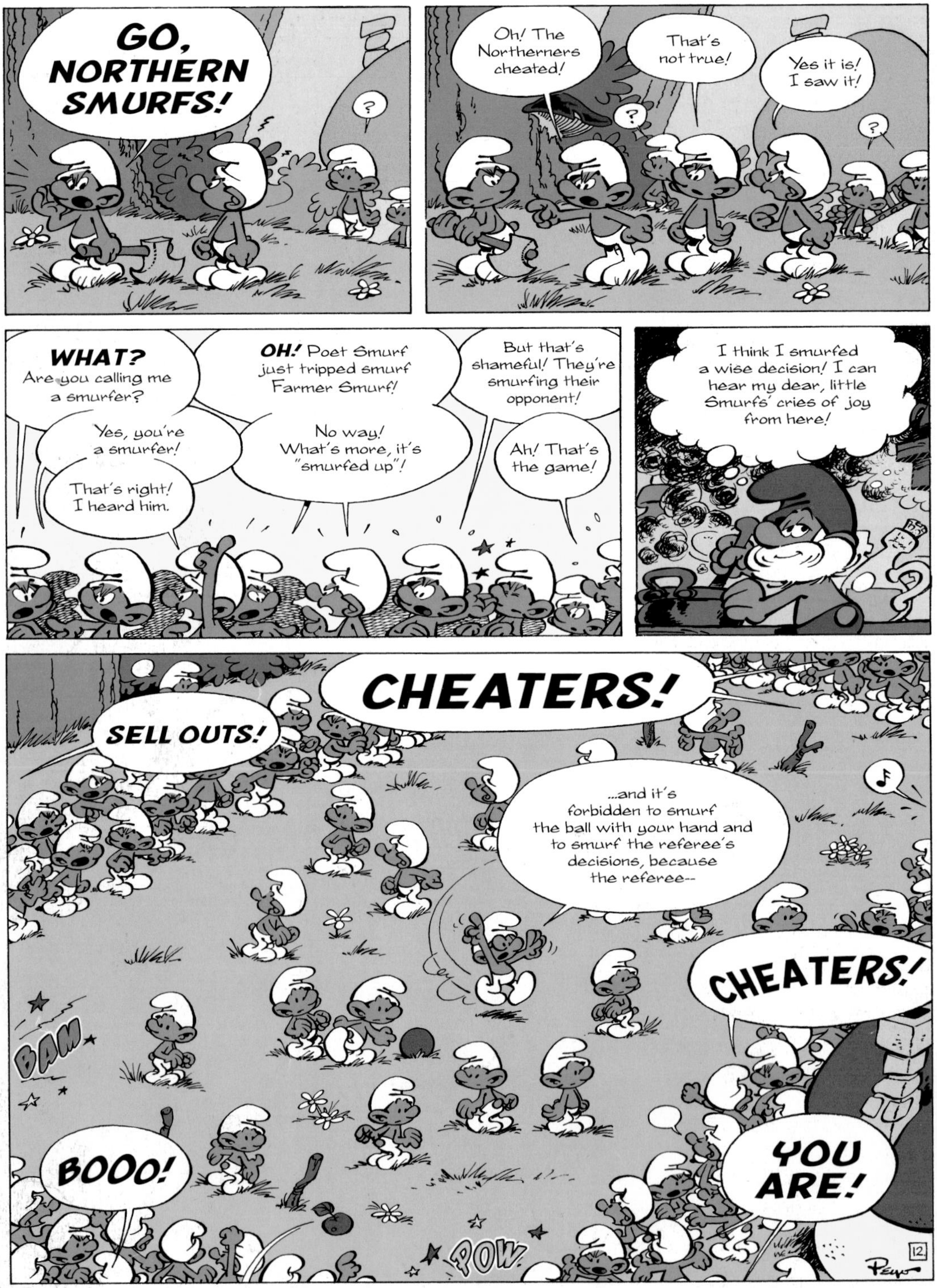
GO, NORTHERN SMURFS!
?
Oh! The Northerners cheated!
That's not true!
?
Yes it is! I saw it!
?
WHAT? Are you calling me a smurfer?
Yes, you're a smurfer!
That's right! I heard him.
OH! Poet Smurf just tripped smurf Farmer Smurf!
No way! What's more, it's "smurfed up"!
But that's shameful! They're smurfing their opponent!
Ah! That's the game!
I think I smurfed a wise decision! I can hear my dear, little Smurfs' cries of joy from here!
CHEATERS!
SELL OUTS!
...and it's forbidden to smurf the ball with your hand and to smurf the referee's decisions, because the referee--
CHEATERS!
BAM
BOOO!
YOU ARE!
POW
12
Peyo

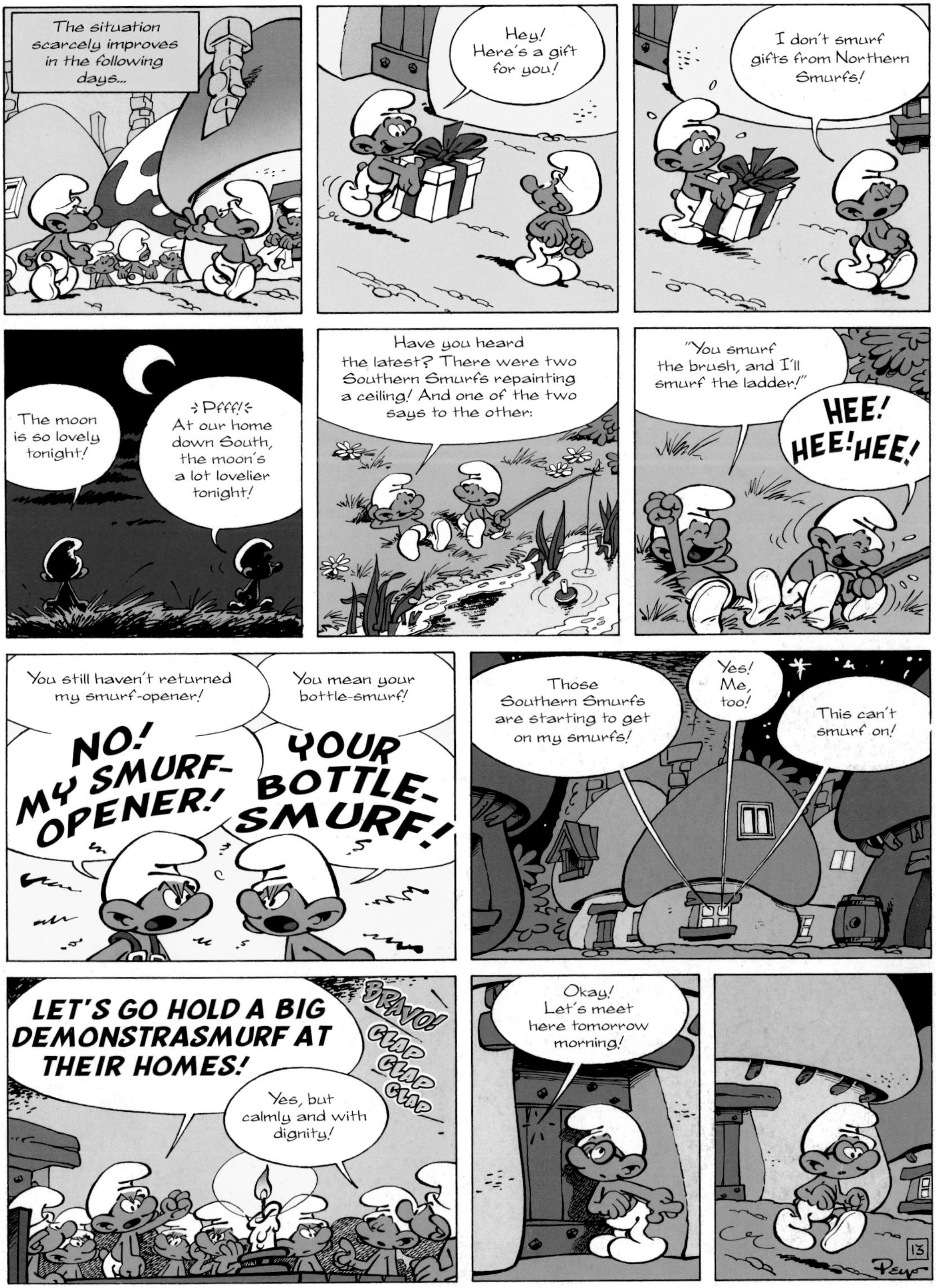
The situation scarcely improves in the following days...
Hey! Here's a gift for you!
I don't smurf gifts from Northern Smurfs!
The moon is so lovely tonight!
Pfff! At our home down South, the moon's a lot lovelier tonight!
Have you heard the latest? There were two Southern Smurfs repainting a ceiling! And one of the two says to the other:
"You smurf the brush, and I'll smurf the ladder!"
HEE! HEE! HEE!
You still haven't returned my smurf-opener!
You mean your bottle-smurf!
NO! MY SMURF-OPENER!
YOUR BOTTLE-SMURF!
Those Southern Smurfs are starting to get on my smurfs!
Yes! Me, too!
This can't smurf on!
LET'S GO HOLD A BIG DEMONSTRASMURF AT THEIR HOMES!
BRAVO!
CLAP CLAP CLAP
Yes, but calmly and with dignity!
Okay! Let's meet here tomorrow morning!
13
Peyo

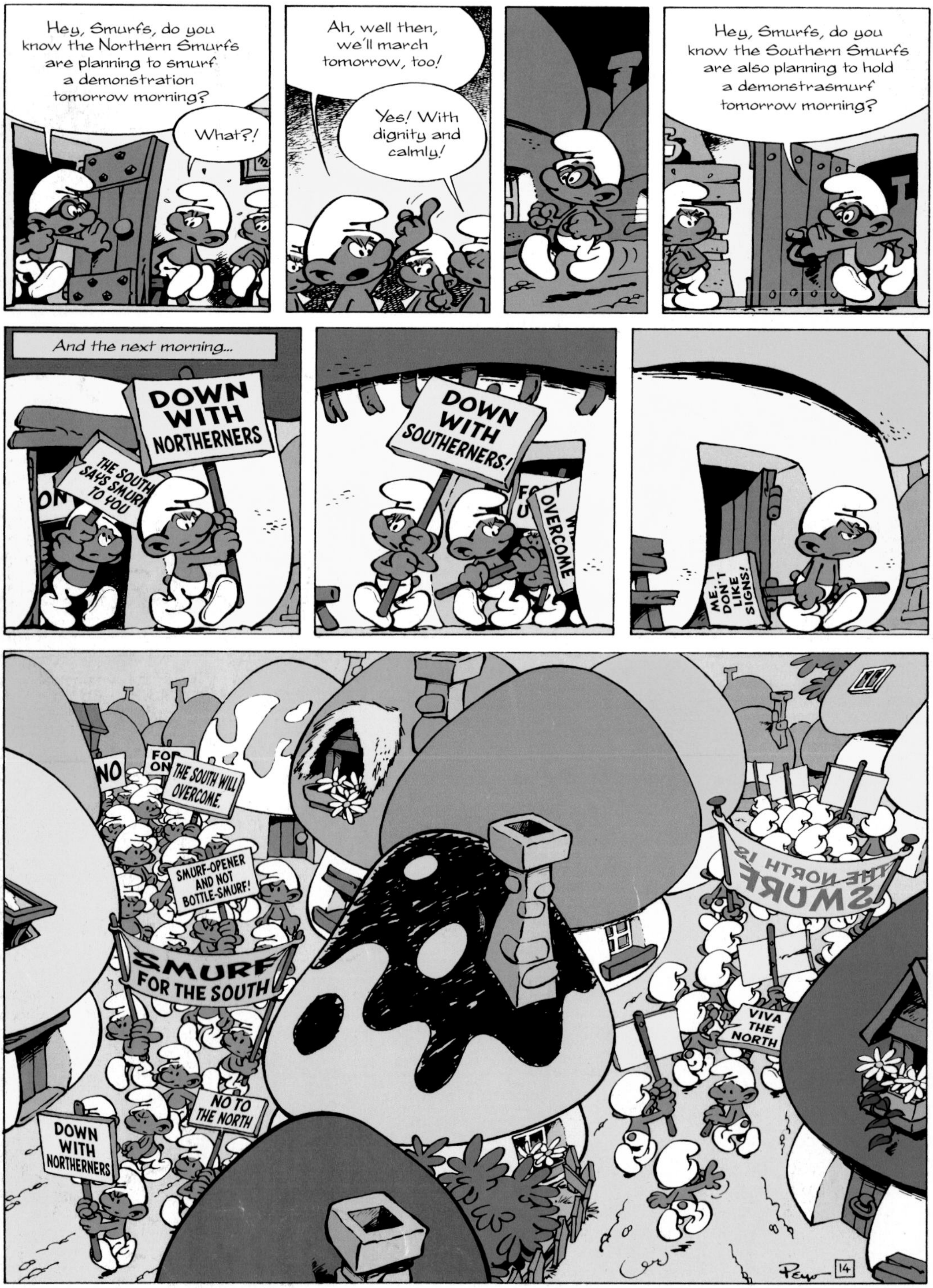

Hey, Smurfs, do you know the Northern Smurfs are planning to smurf a demonstration tomorrow morning?
What?!
Ah, well then, we'll march tomorrow, too!
Yes! With dignity and calmly!
Hey, Smurfs, do you know the Southern Smurfs are also planning to hold a demonstrasmurf tomorrow morning?
And the next morning...
DOWN WITH NORTHERNERS
THE SOUTH SAYS SMURF TO YOU
DOWN WITH SOUTHERNERS!
ME, I DON'T LIKE SIGNS!
THE SOUTH WILL OVERCOME.
SMURF-OPENER AND NOT BOTTLE-SMURF!
SMURF FOR THE SOUTH
THE NORTH IS SMURF
VIVA THE NORTH
NO TO THE NORTH
DOWN WITH NORTHERNERS
Peyo 14

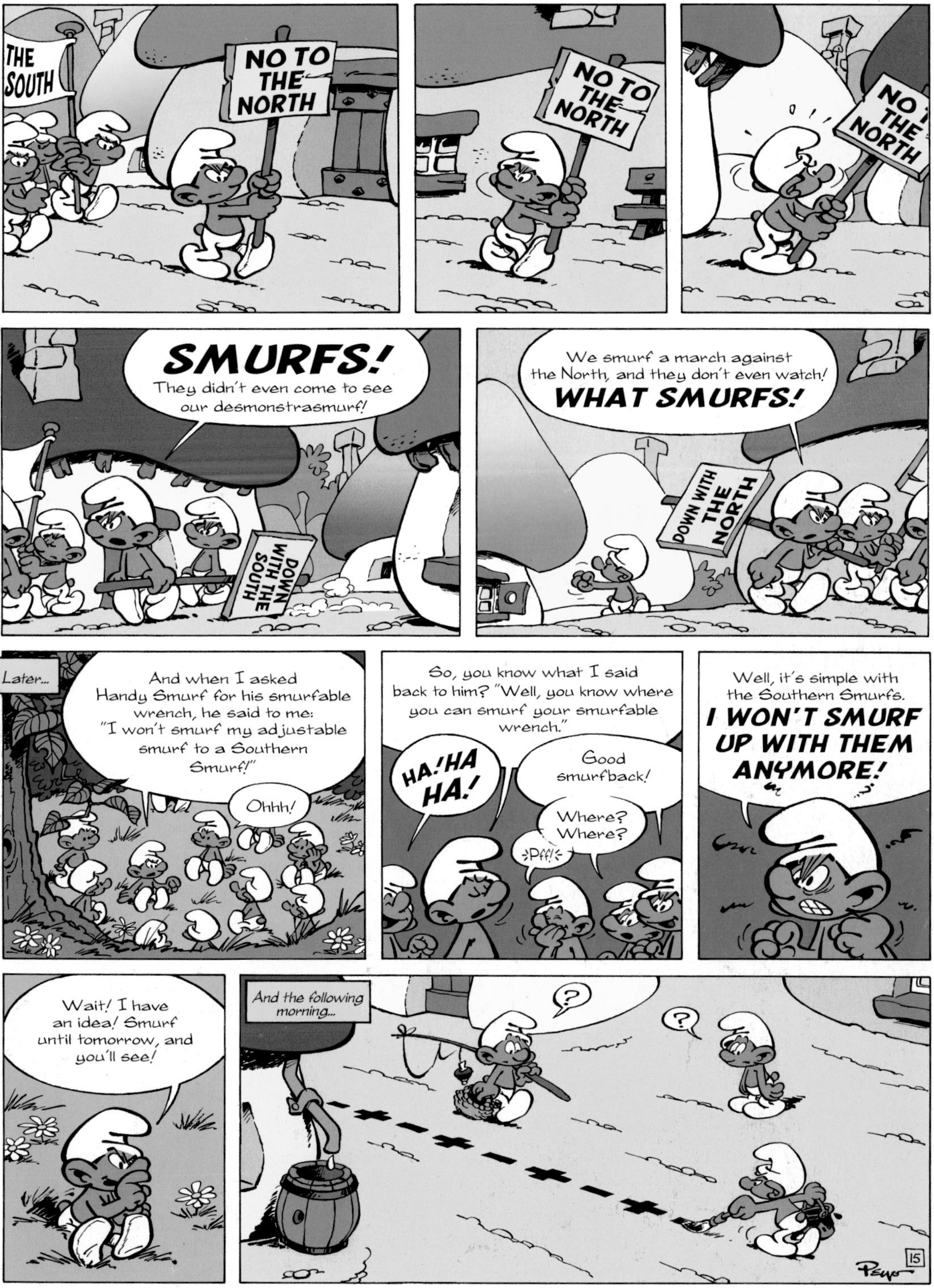
THE SOUTH
NO TO THE NORTH
NO TO THE NORTH
NO TO THE NORTH
SMURFS! They didn't even come to see our desmonstrasmurf!
DOWN WITH THE SOUTH
We smurf a march against the North, and they don't even watch! WHAT SMURFS!
DOWN WITH THE NORTH
Later...
And when I asked Handy Smurf for his smurfable wrench, he said to me: "I won't smurf my adjustable smurf to a Southern Smurf!"
Ohhh!
So, you know what I said back to him? "Well, you know where you can smurf your smurfable wrench."
HA! HA HA!
Good smurfback!
Where? Where?
Pff!
Well, it's simple with the Southern Smurfs. I WON'T SMURF UP WITH THEM ANYMORE!
Wait! I have an idea! Smurf until tomorrow, and you'll see!
And the following morning...
?
?
15
Peyo

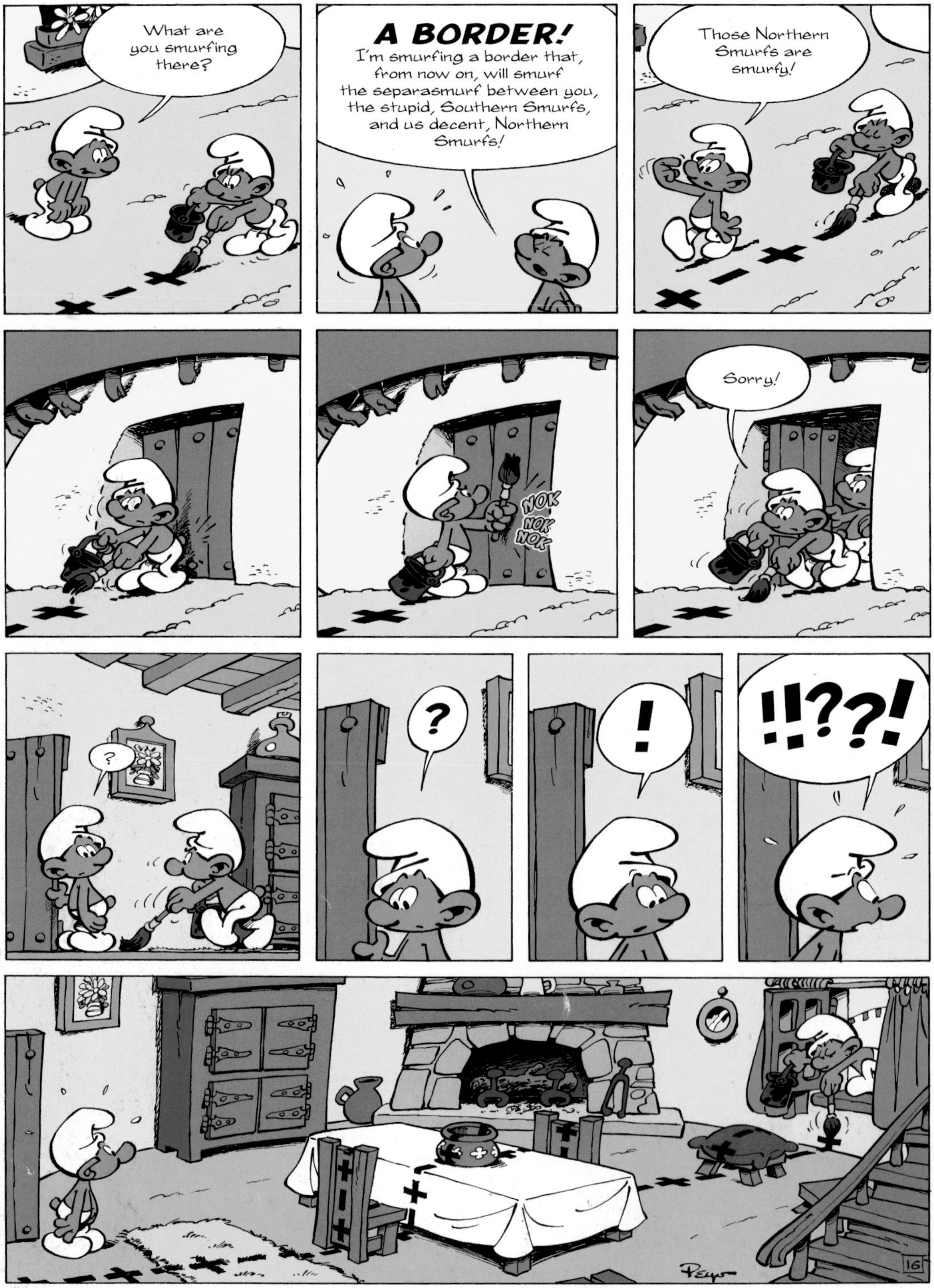
What are you smurfing there?
A BORDER!
I'm smurfing a border that, from now on, will smurf the separasmurf between you, the stupid, Southern Smurfs, and us decent, Northern Smurfs!
Those Northern Smurfs are smurfy!
NOK NOK NOK
Sorry!
?
?
!
!!??!
16

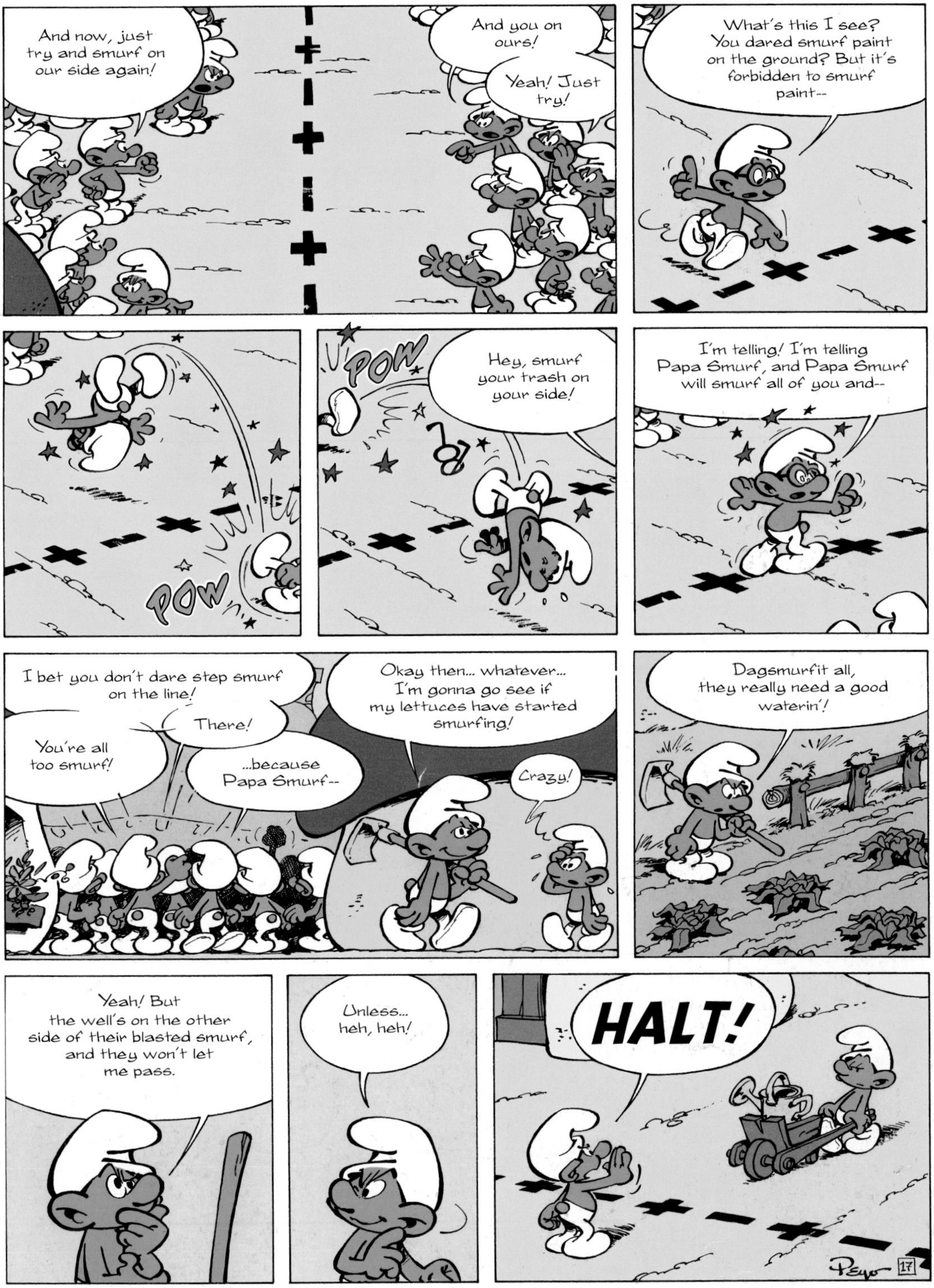

And now, just try and smurf on our side again!
And you on ours!
Yeah! Just try!
What's this I see? You dared smurf paint on the ground? But it's forbidden to smurf paint--
POW
POW
Hey, smurf your trash on your side!
I'm telling! I'm telling Papa Smurf, and Papa Smurf will smurf all of you and--
I bet you don't dare step smurf on the line!
There!
You're all too smurf!
...because Papa Smurf--
Okay then... whatever... I'm gonna go see if my lettuces have started smurfing!
Crazy!
Dagsmurfit all, they really need a good waterin'!
Yeah! But the well's on the other side of their blasted smurf, and they won't let me pass.
Unless... heh, heh!
HALT!
Peyo
17

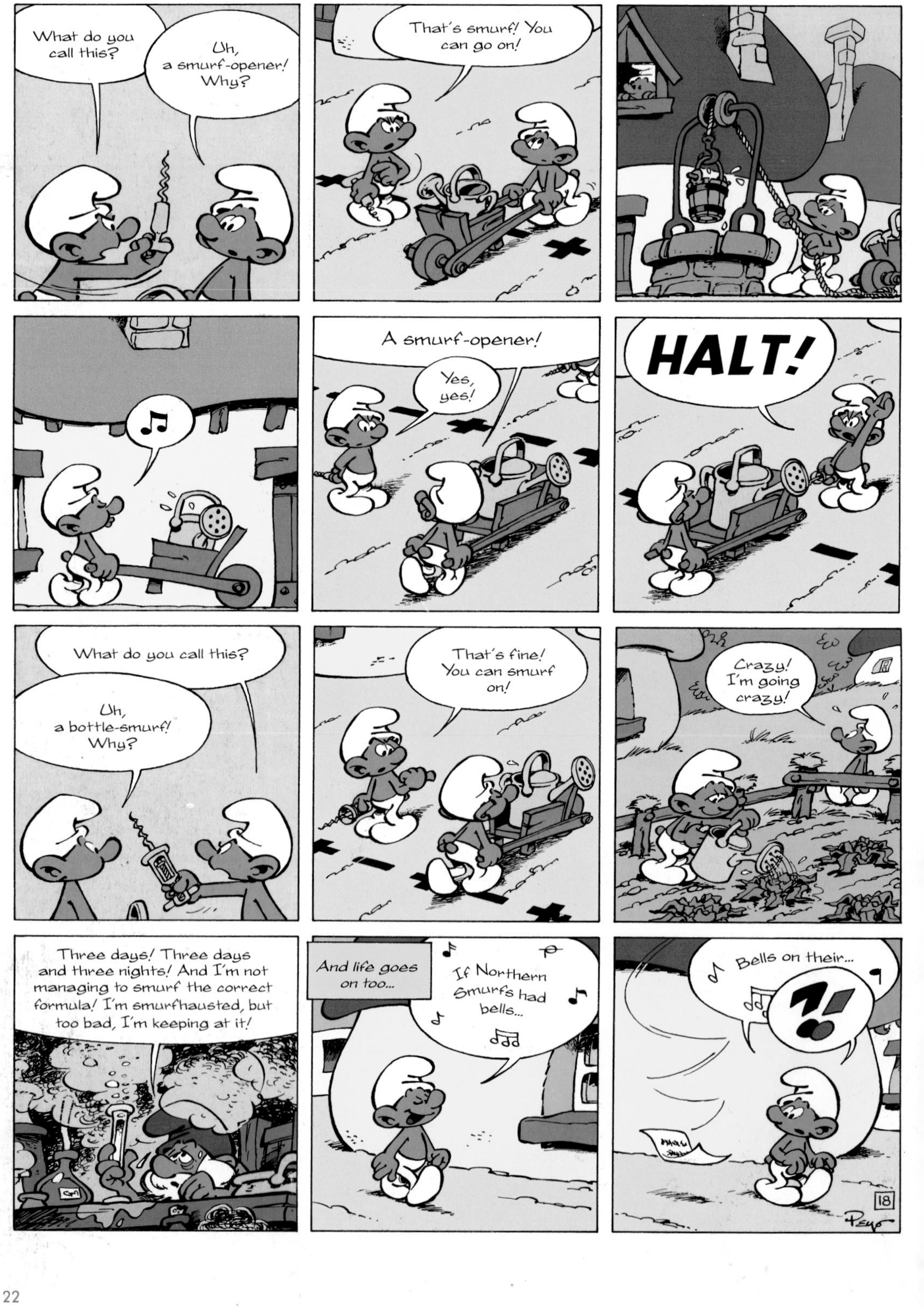
What do you call this?
Uh, a smurf-opener! Why?
That's smurf! You can go on!
A smurf-opener!
Yes, yes!
HALT!
What do you call this?
Uh, a bottle-smurf! Why?
That's fine! You can smurf on!
Crazy! I'm going crazy!
Three days! Three days and three nights! And I'm not managing to smurf the correct formula! I'm smurfhausted, but too bad, I'm keeping at it!
And life goes on too...
If Northern Smurfs had bells...
Bells on their...
18
Peyo

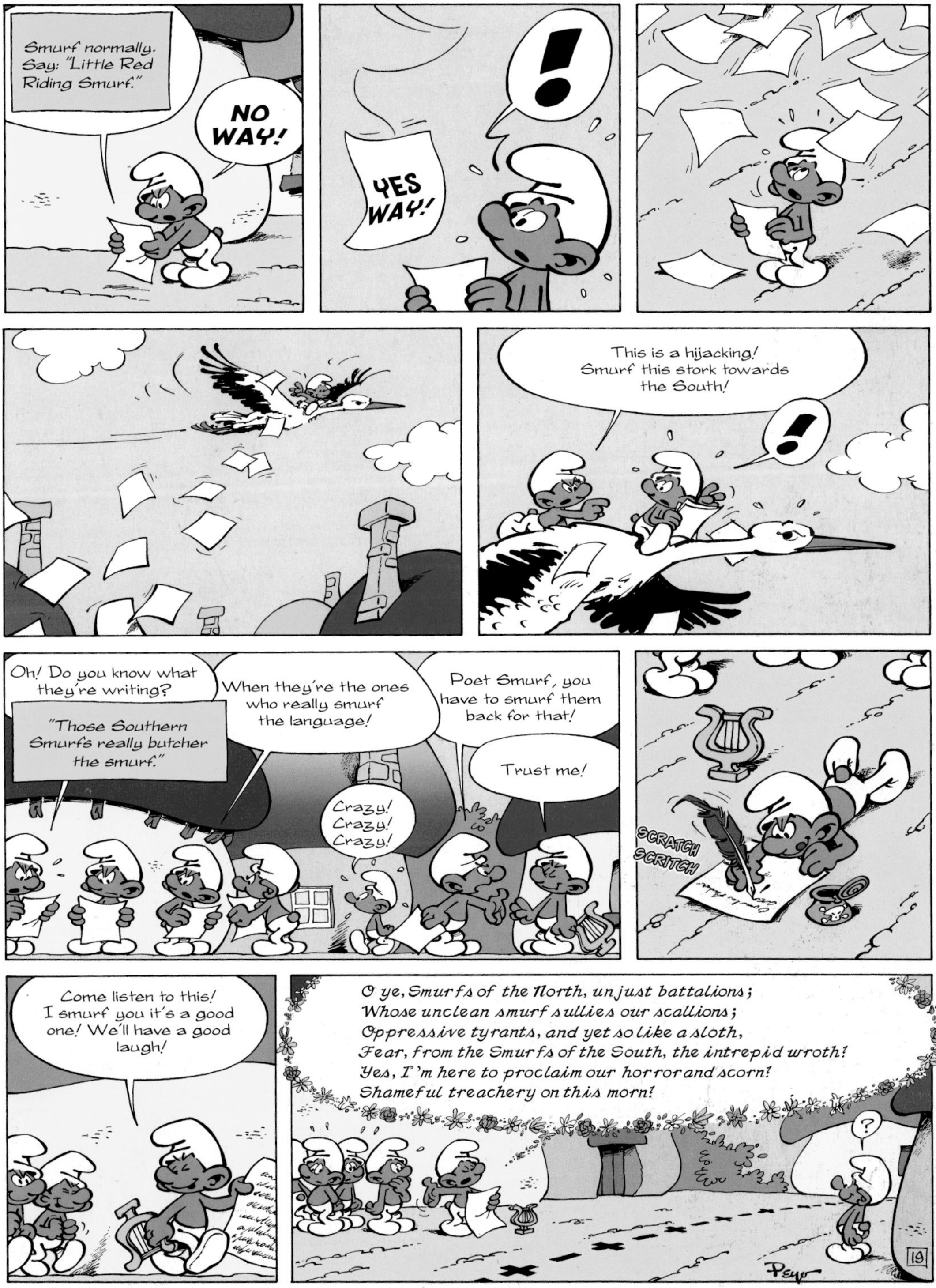
Smurf normally. Say: "Little Red Riding Smurf."
NO WAY!
!
YES WAY!
This is a hijacking! Smurf this stork towards the South!
!
Oh! Do you know what they're writing?
"Those Southern Smurfs really butcher the smurf."
When they're the ones who really smurf the language!
Poet Smurf, you have to smurf them back for that!
Trust me!
Crazy! Crazy! Crazy!
SCRATCH SCRITCH
Come listen to this! I smurf you it's a good one! We'll have a good laugh!
O ye, Smurfs of the North, unjust battalions;
Whose unclean smurf sullies our scallions;
Oppressive tyrants, and yet so like a sloth,
Fear, from the Smurfs of the South, the intrepid wroth!
Yes, I'm here to proclaim our horror and scorn!
Shameful treachery on this morn!
?
Peyo
19

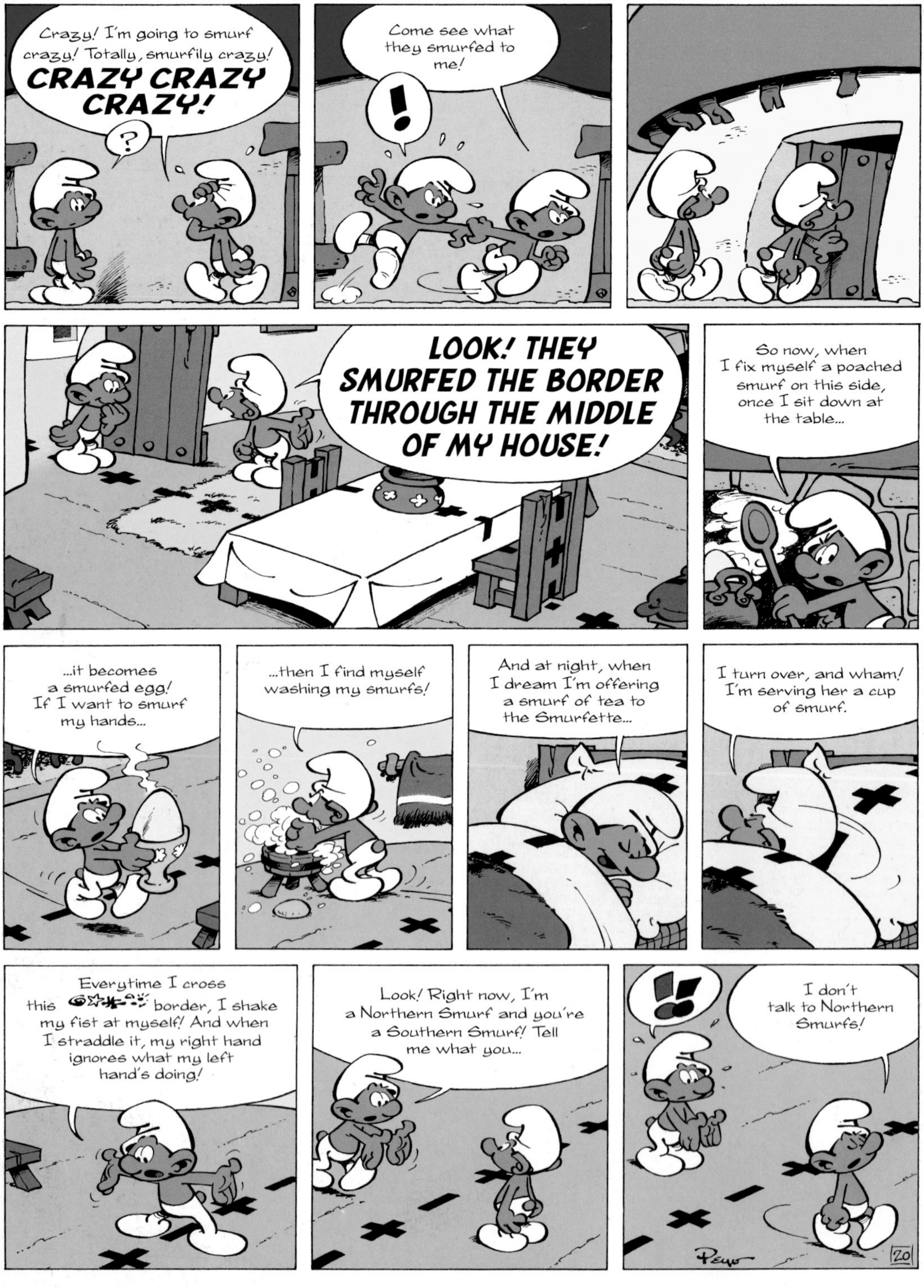

Crazy! I'm going to smurf crazy! Totally, smurfily crazy! CRAZY CRAZY CRAZY!
?
!
Come see what they smurfed to me!
LOOK! THEY SMURFED THE BORDER THROUGH THE MIDDLE OF MY HOUSE!
So now, when I fix myself a poached smurf on this side, once I sit down at the table...
...it becomes a smurfed egg! If I want to smurf my hands...
...then I find myself washing my smurfs!
And at night, when I dream I'm offering a smurf of tea to the Smurfette...
I turn over, and wham! I'm serving her a cup of smurf.
Everytime I cross this border, I shake my fist at myself! And when I straddle it, my right hand ignores what my left hand's doing!
Look! Right now, I'm a Northern Smurf and you're a Southern Smurf! Tell me what you...
!!
I don't talk to Northern Smurfs!
20

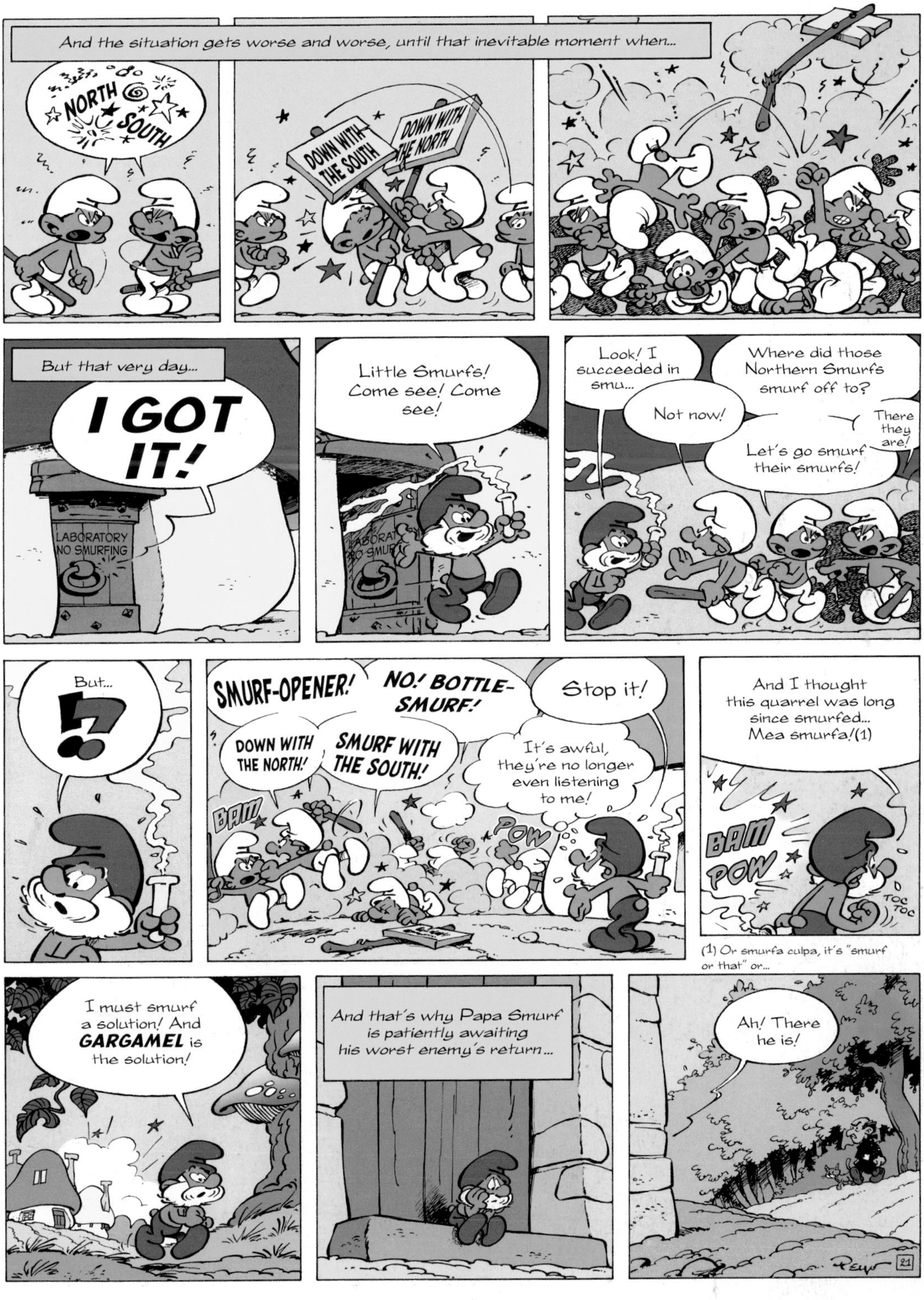
And the situation gets worse and worse, until that inevitable moment when...
NORTH
SOUTH
DOWN WITH THE SOUTH
DOWN WITH THE NORTH
But that very day...
I GOT IT!
LABORATORY NO SMURFING
Little Smurfs! Come see! Come see!
Look! I succeeded in smu...
Not now!
Where did those Northern Smurfs smurf off to?
There they are!
Let's go smurf their smurfs!
But...
SMURF-OPENER!
NO! BOTTLE-SMURF!
Stop it!
DOWN WITH THE NORTH!
SMURF WITH THE SOUTH!
It's awful, they're no longer even listening to me!
BAM
POW
And I thought this quarrel was long since smurfed... Mea smurfa!(1)
BAM
POW
TOC TOC
(1) Or smurfa culpa, it's "smurf or that" or...
I must smurf a solution! And GARGAMEL is the solution!
And that's why Papa Smurf is patiently awaiting his worst enemy's return...
Ah! There he is!
21

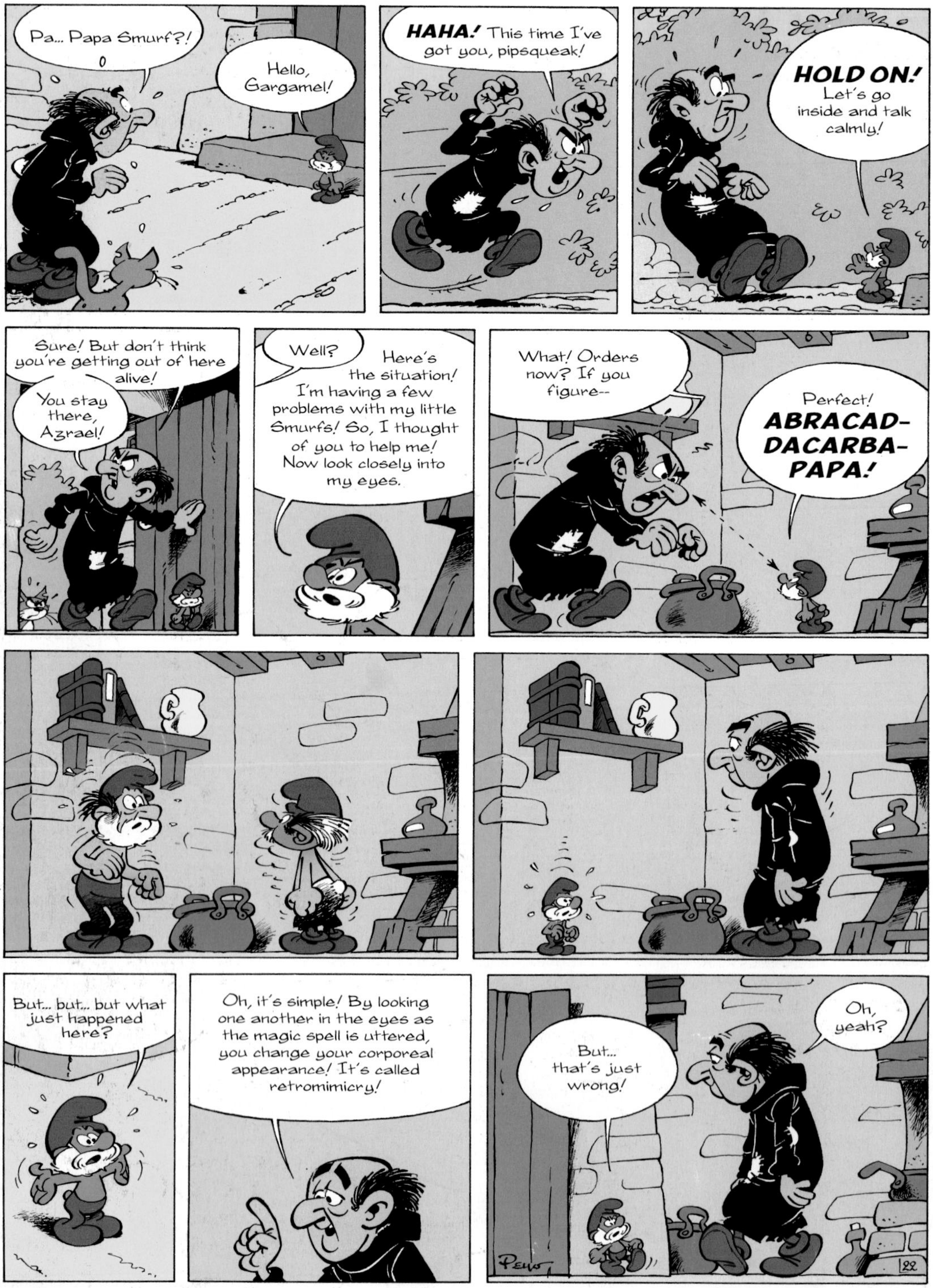
Pa... Papa Smurf?!
Hello, Gargamel!
HAHA! This time I've got you, pipsqueak!
HOLD ON! Let's go inside and talk calmly!
Sure! But don't think you're getting out of here alive!
You stay there, Azrael!
Well?
Here's the situation! I'm having a few problems with my little Smurfs! So, I thought of you to help me! Now look closely into my eyes.
What! Orders now? If you figure--
Perfect! ABRACAD-DACARBA-PAPA!
But... but... but what just happened here?
Oh, it's simple! By looking one another in the eyes as the magic spell is uttered, you change your corporeal appearance! It's called retromimicry!
But... that's just wrong!
Oh, yeah?
22

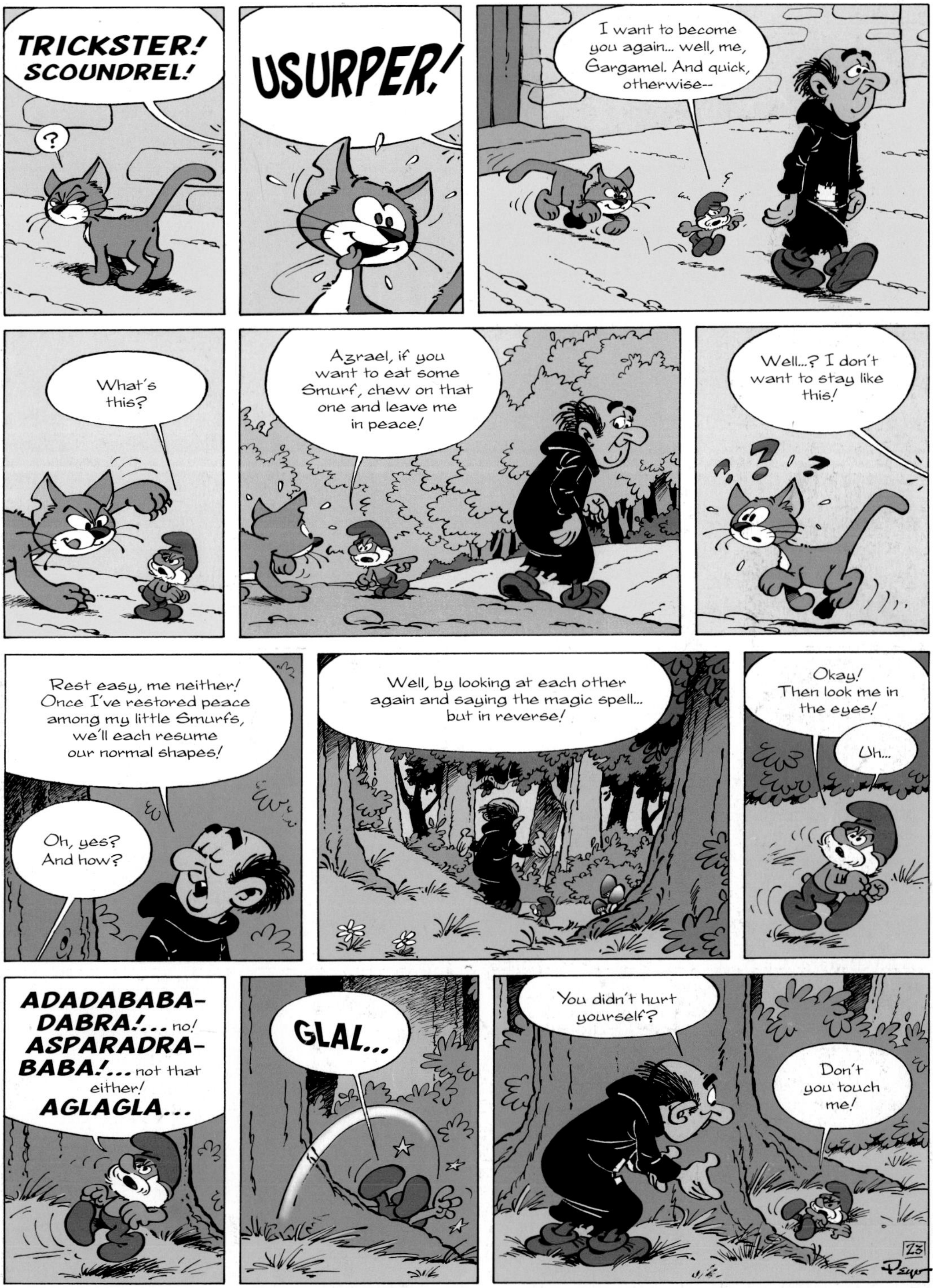
TRICKSTER! SCOUNDREL!
?
USURPER!
I want to become you again... well, me, Gargamel. And quick, otherwise--
What's this?
Azrael, if you want to eat some Smurf, chew on that one and leave me in peace!
Well...? I don't want to stay like this!
Rest easy, me neither! Once I've restored peace among my little Smurfs, we'll each resume our normal shapes!
Oh, yes? And how?
Well, by looking at each other again and saying the magic spell... but in reverse!
Okay! Then look me in the eyes!
Uh...
ADADABABA-DABRA!... no! ASPARADRA-BABA!... not that either! AGLAGLA...
GLAL...
You didn't hurt yourself?
Don't you touch me!
23

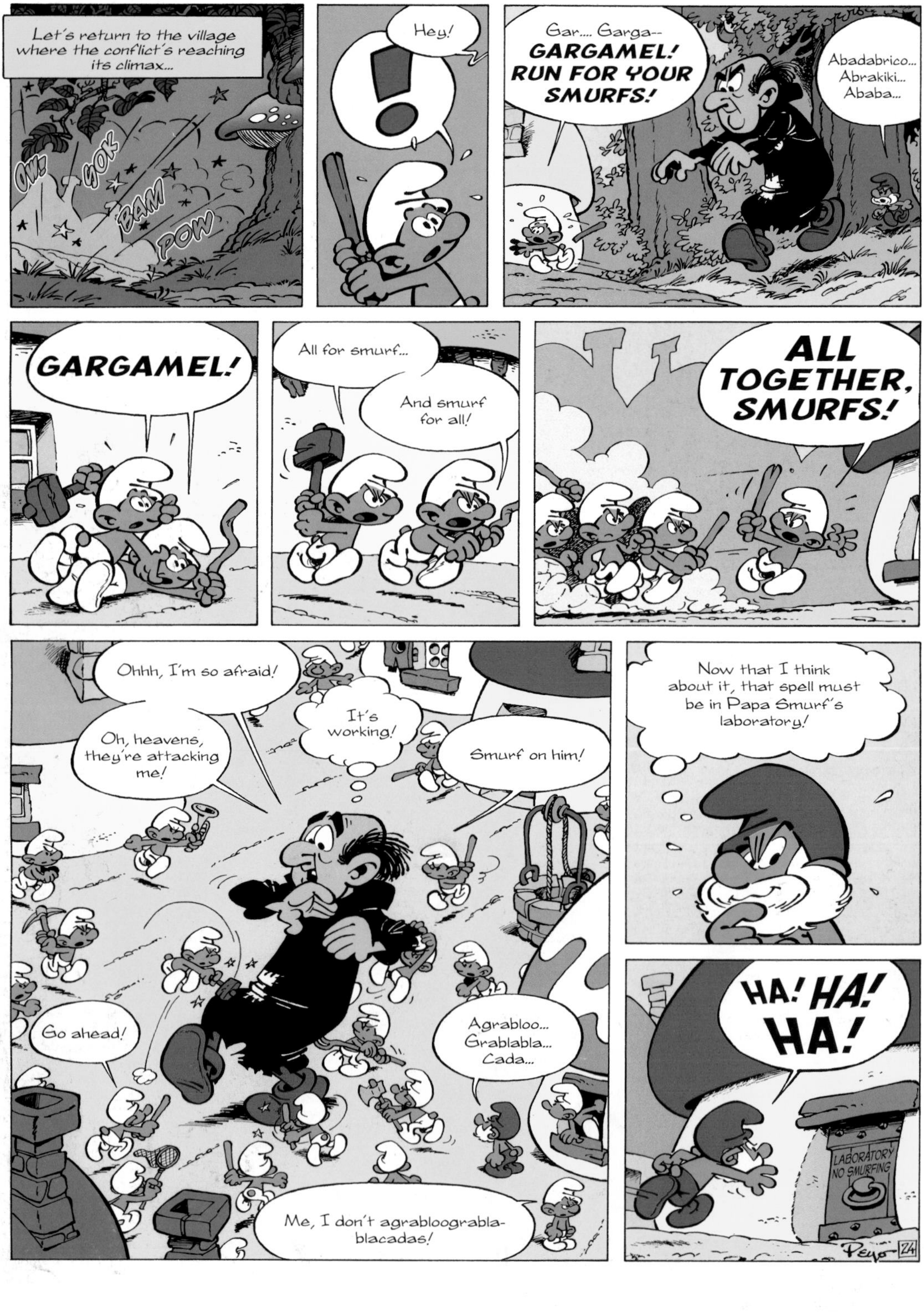
Let's return to the village where the conflict's reaching its climax...
OW!
SOK
BAM
POW
Hey!
Gar.... Garga--
GARGAMEL! RUN FOR YOUR SMURFS!
Abadabrico... Abrakiki... Ababa...
GARGAMEL!
All for smurf...
And smurf for all!
ALL TOGETHER, SMURFS!
Ohhh, I'm so afraid!
Oh, heavens, they're attacking me!
It's working!
Smurf on him!
Go ahead!
Agrabloo... Grablabla... Cada...
Me, I don't agrabloograbla-blacadas!
Now that I think about it, that spell must be in Papa Smurf's laboratory!
HA! HA! HA!
LABORATORY NO SMURFING
Peyo 24

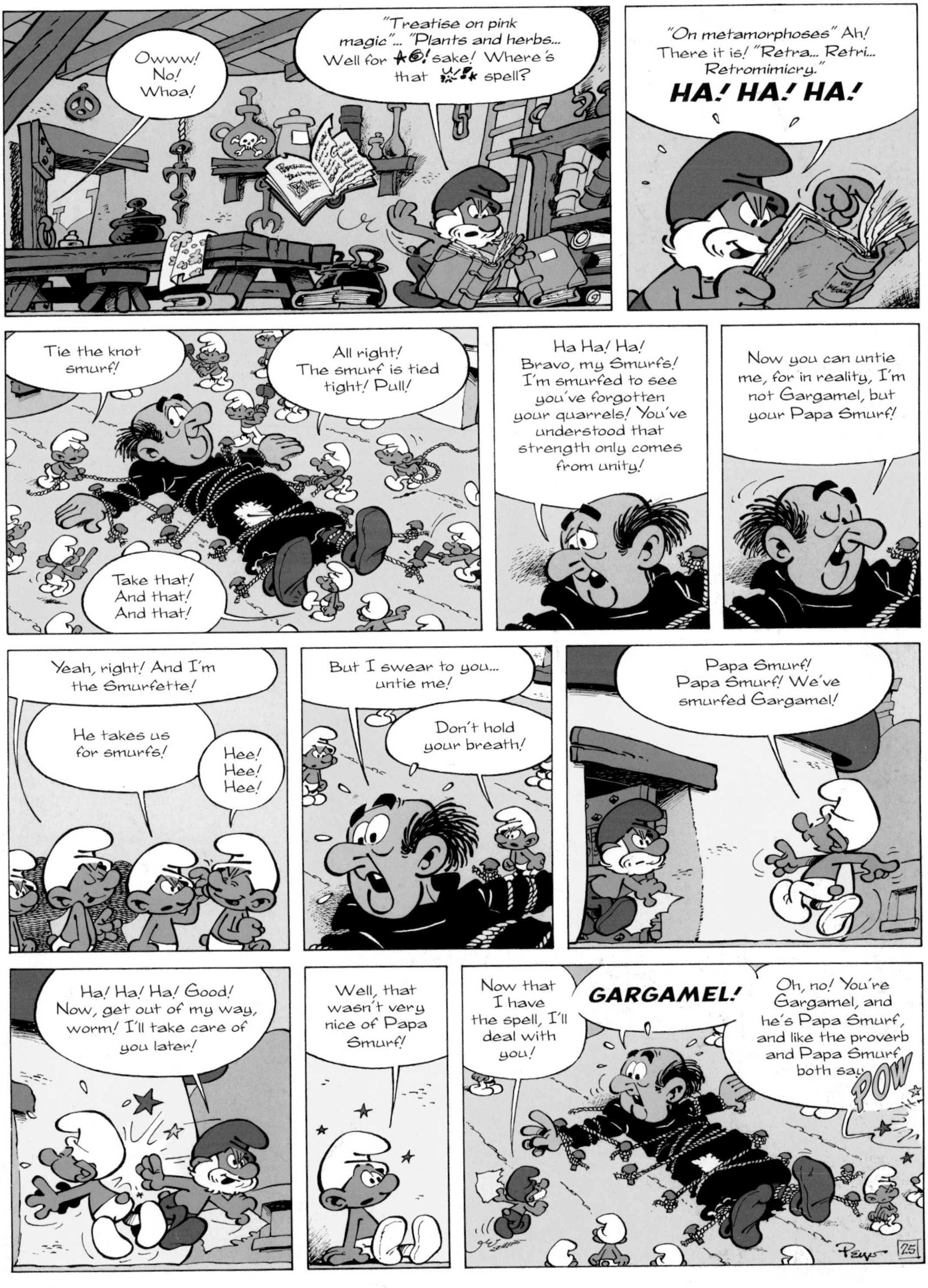
Owww! No! Whoa!
"Treatise on pink magic"... "Plants and herbs... Well for sake! Where's that spell?
"On metamorphoses" Ah! There it is! "Retra... Retri... Retromimicry."
HA! HA! HA!
Tie the knot smurf!
All right! The smurf is tied tight! Pull!
Take that! And that! And that!
Ha Ha! Ha! Bravo, my Smurfs! I'm smurfed to see you've forgotten your quarrels! You've understood that strength only comes from unity!
Now you can untie me, for in reality, I'm not Gargamel, but your Papa Smurf!
Yeah, right! And I'm the Smurfette!
He takes us for smurfs!
Hee! Hee! Hee!
But I swear to you... untie me!
Don't hold your breath!
Papa Smurf! Papa Smurf! We've smurfed Gargamel!
Ha! Ha! Ha! Good! Now, get out of my way, worm! I'll take care of you later!
Well, that wasn't very nice of Papa Smurf!
Now that I have the spell, I'll deal with you!
GARGAMEL!
Oh, no! You're Gargamel, and he's Papa Smurf, and like the proverb and Papa Smurf both say
POW
Peyo
25

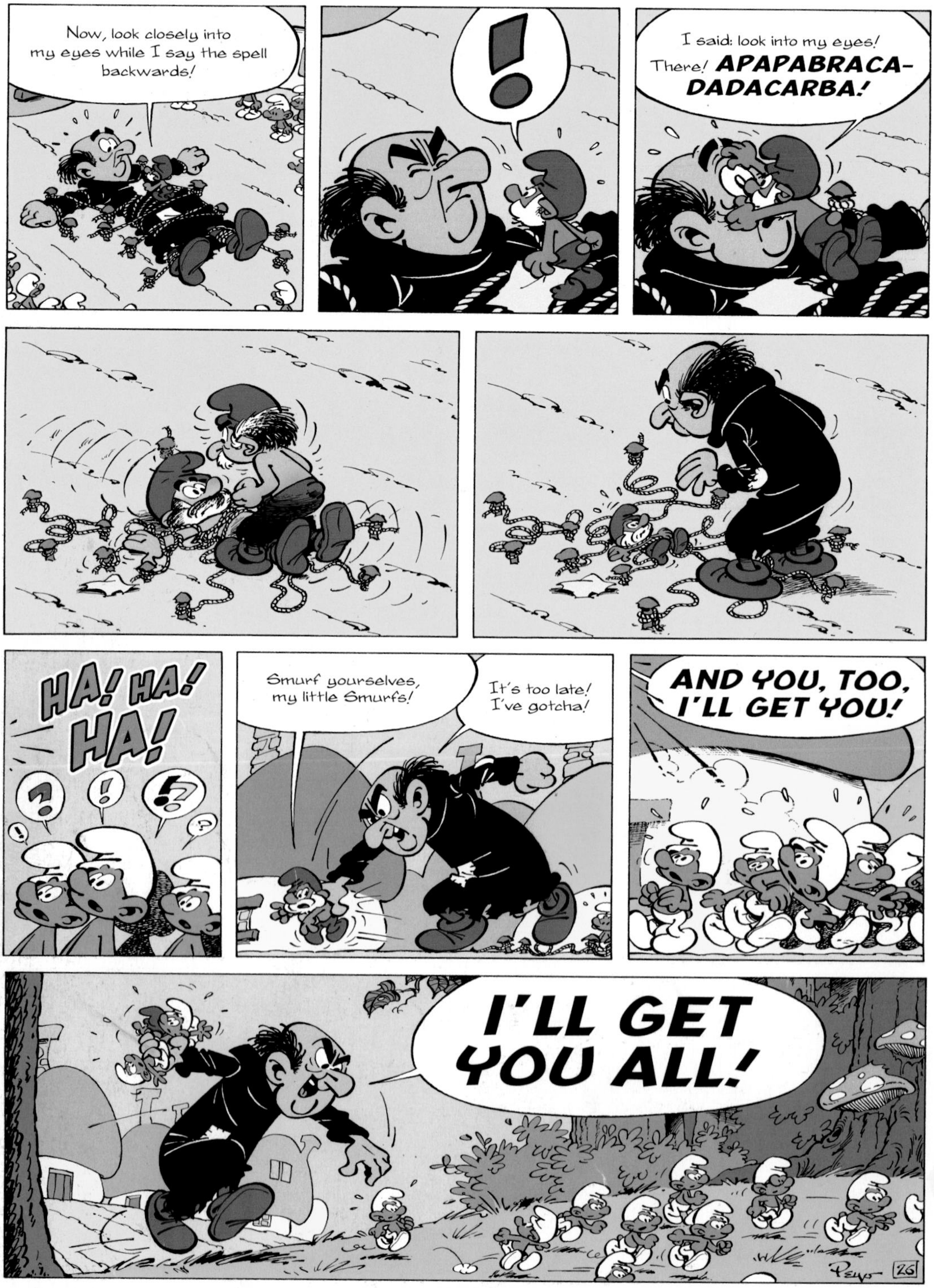
Now, look closely into my eyes while I say the spell backwards!
!
I said: look into my eyes! There! APAPABRACA-DADACARBA!
HA! HA! HA!
?
!
!?
!
?
Smurf yourselves, my little Smurfs!
It's too late! I've gotcha!
AND YOU, TOO, I'LL GET YOU!
I'LL GET YOU ALL!
Peyo
26

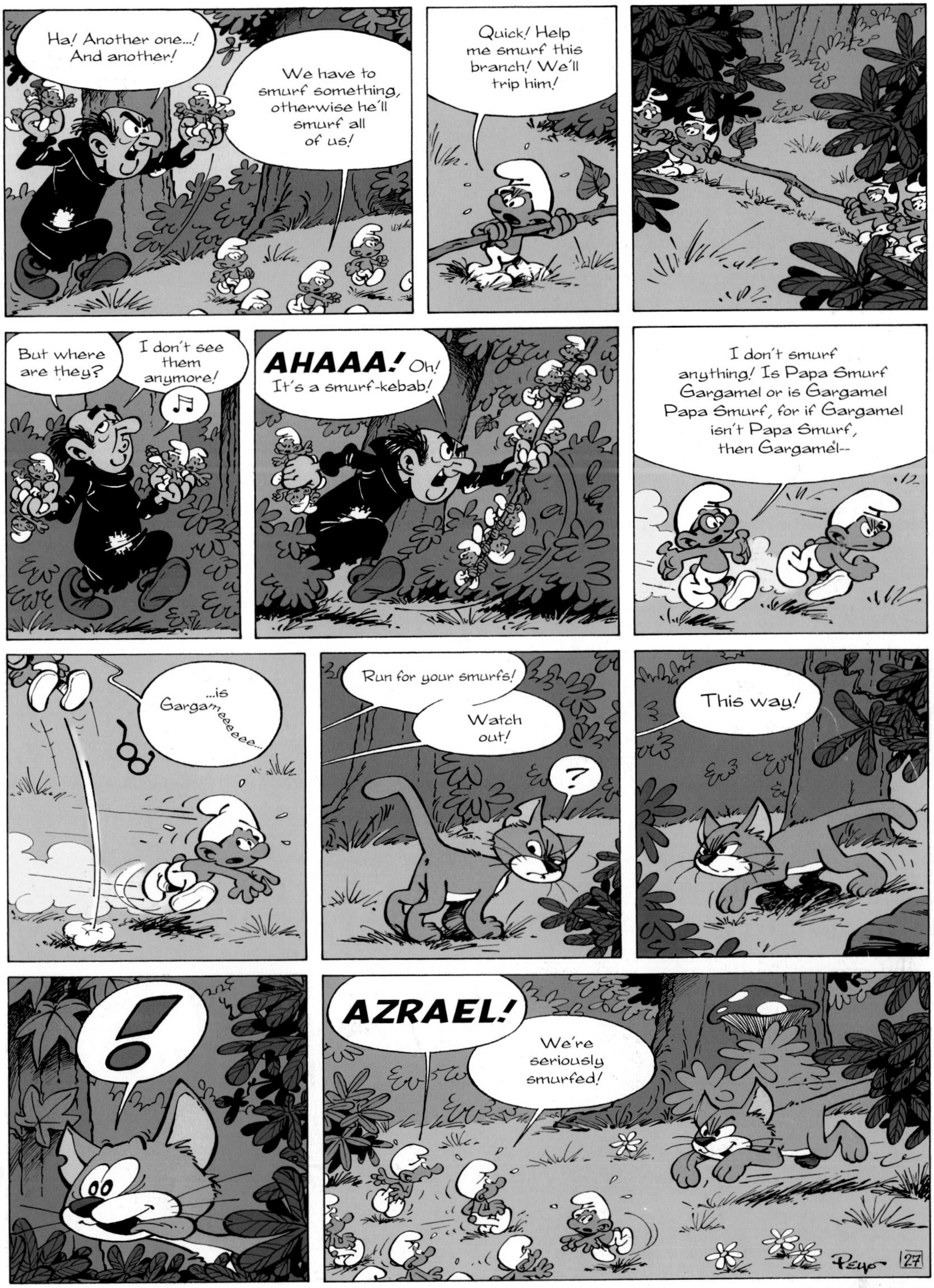

Ha! Another one...! And another!
We have to smurf something, otherwise he'll smurf all of us!
Quick! Help me smurf this branch! We'll trip him!
But where are they?
I don't see them anymore!
AHAAA! Oh! It's a smurf-kebab!
I don't smurf anything! Is Papa Smurf Gargamel or is Gargamel Papa Smurf, for if Gargamel isn't Papa Smurf, then Gargamel--
...is Gargameeeeee...
Run for your smurfs!
Watch out!
?
This way!
!
AZRAEL!
We're seriously smurfed!
Peyo
27

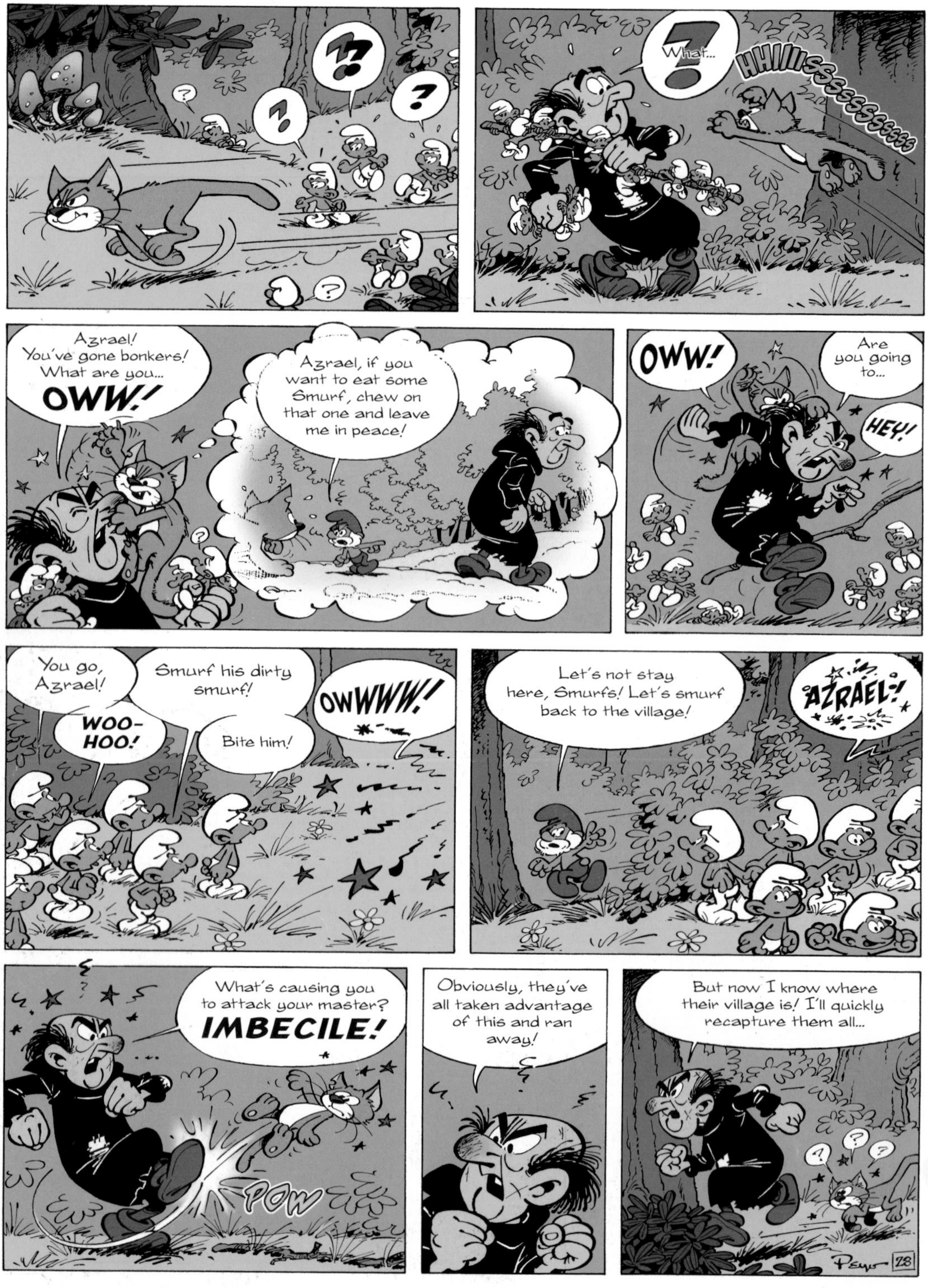
?
?
?
?
?
What...
HHIIIISSSSSSSSSSS
Azrael! You've gone bonkers! What are you... OWW!
Azrael, if you want to eat some Smurf, chew on that one and leave me in peace!
OWW!
Are you going to...
HEY!
You go, Azrael!
Smurf his dirty smurf!
WOO-HOO!
Bite him!
OWWWW!
Let's not stay here, Smurfs! Let's smurf back to the village!
AZRAEL!
What's causing you to attack your master? IMBECILE!
POW
Obviously, they've all taken advantage of this and ran away!
But now I know where their village is! I'll quickly recapture them all...
28

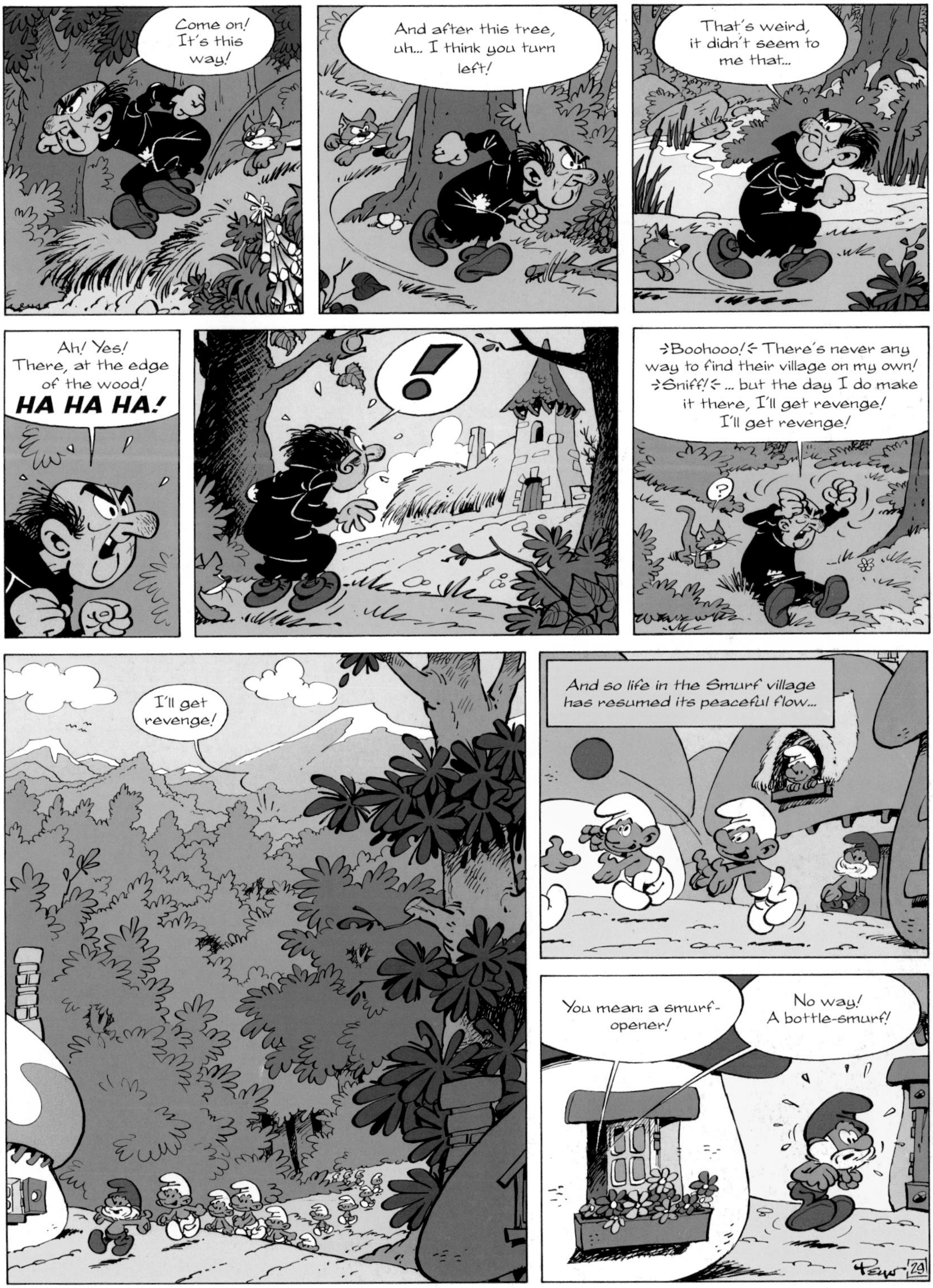
Come on! It's this way!
And after this tree, uh... I think you turn left!
That's weird, it didn't seem to me that...
Ah! Yes! There, at the edge of the wood! HA HA HA!
!
>Boohooo!< There's never any way to find their village on my own! >Sniff!< ... but the day I do make it there, I'll get revenge! I'll get revenge!
?
I'll get revenge!
And so life in the Smurf village has resumed its peaceful flow...
You mean: a smurf-opener!
No way! A bottle-smurf!

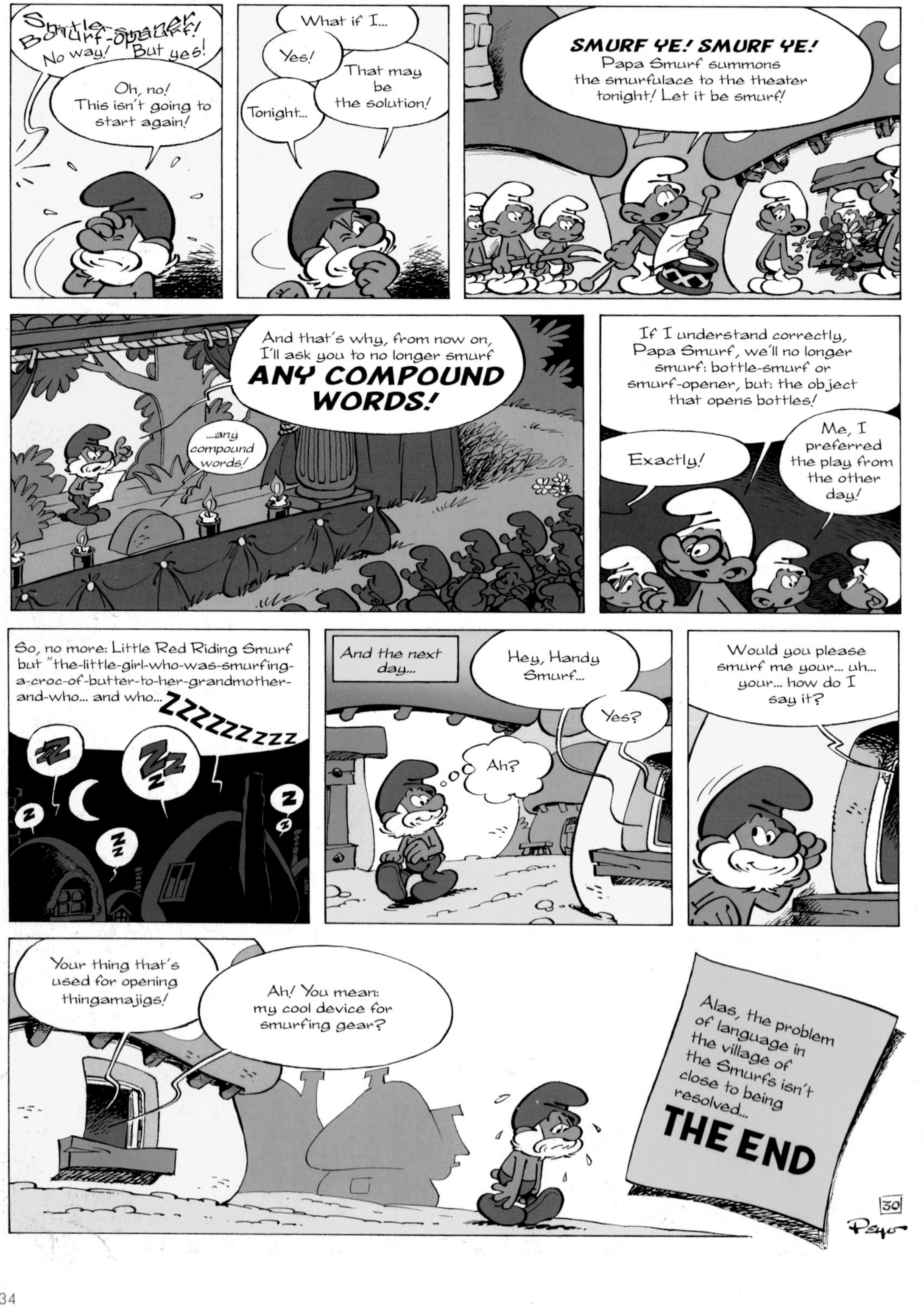

No way! But yes!
Oh, no! This isn't going to start again!
What if I...
Yes!
Tonight...
That may be the solution!
SMURF YE! SMURF YE!
Papa Smurf summons the smurfulace to the theater tonight! Let it be smurf!
And that's why, from now on, I'll ask you to no longer smurf
ANY COMPOUND WORDS!
...any compound words!
If I understand correctly, Papa Smurf, we'll no longer smurf: bottle-smurf or smurf-opener, but: the object that opens bottles!
Exactly!
Me, I preferred the play from the other day!
So, no more: Little Red Riding Smurf but "the-little-girl-who-was-smurfing-a-croc-of-butter-to-her-grandmother-and-who... and who...
ZZZZZZZzzz
And the next day...
Hey, Handy Smurf...
Yes?
Ah?
Would you please smurf me your... uh... your... how do I say it?
Your thing that's used for opening thingamajigs!
Ah! You mean: my cool device for smurfing gear?
Alas, the problem of language in the village of the Smurfs isn't close to being resolved...
THE END
30
Peyo

# THE PAINTER SMURF

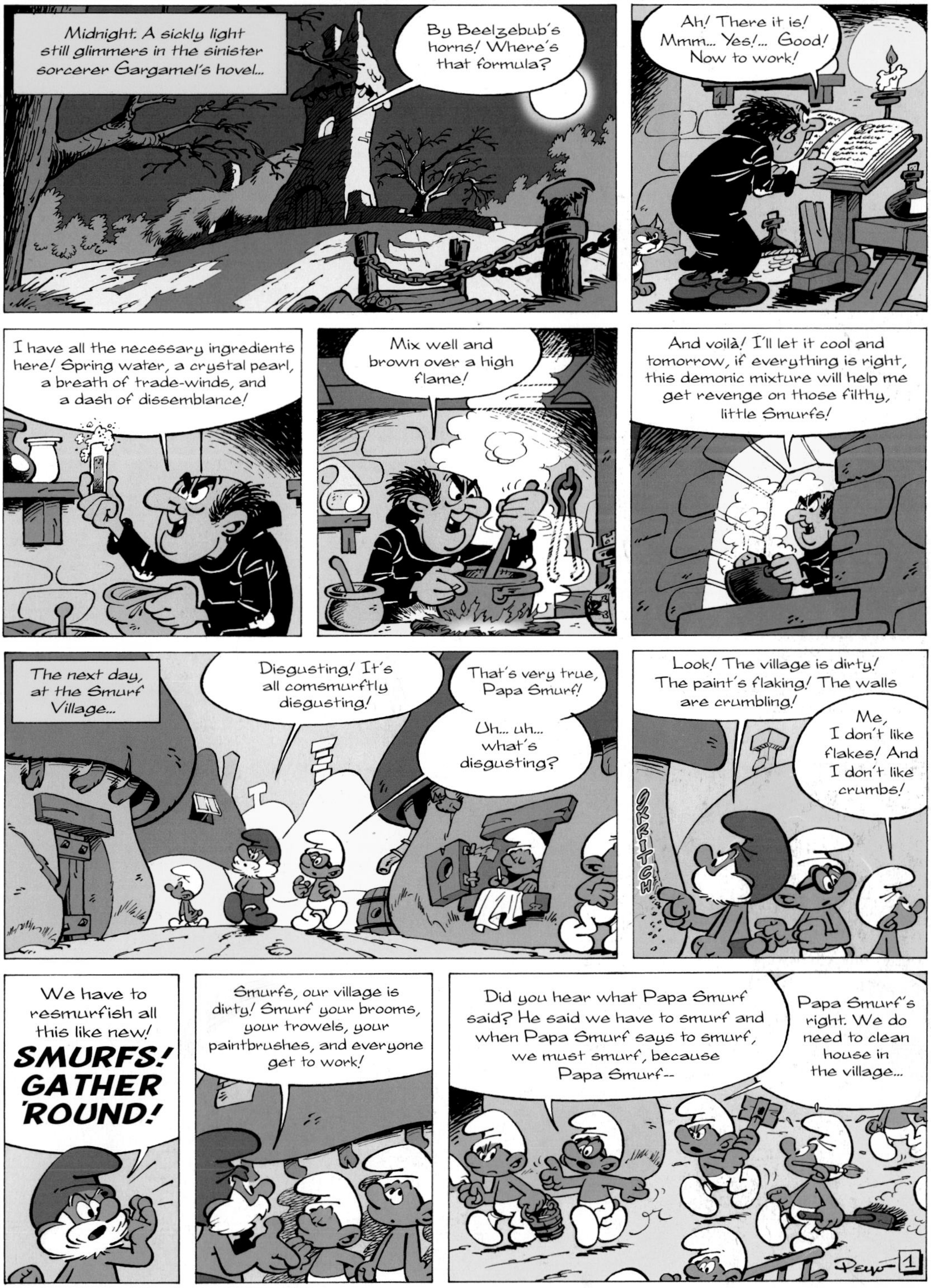
Midnight. A sickly light still glimmers in the sinister sorcerer Gargamel's hovel...
By Beelzebub's horns! Where's that formula?
Ah! There it is! Mmm... Yes!... Good! Now to work!
I have all the necessary ingredients here! Spring water, a crystal pearl, a breath of trade-winds, and a dash of dissemblance!
Mix well and brown over a high flame!
And voilà! I'll let it cool and tomorrow, if everything is right, this demonic mixture will help me get revenge on those filthy, little Smurfs!
The next day, at the Smurf Village...
Disgusting! It's all comsmurftly disgusting!
That's very true, Papa Smurf!
Uh... uh... what's disgusting?
Look! The village is dirty! The paint's flaking! The walls are crumbling!
SKRITCH
Me, I don't like flakes! And I don't like crumbs!
We have to resmurfish all this like new!
SMURFS! GATHER 'ROUND!
Smurfs, our village is dirty! Smurf your brooms, your trowels, your paintbrushes, and everyone get to work!
Did you hear what Papa Smurf said? He said we have to smurf and when Papa Smurf says to smurf, we must smurf, because Papa Smurf--
Papa Smurf's right. We do need to clean house in the village...
Peyo
1

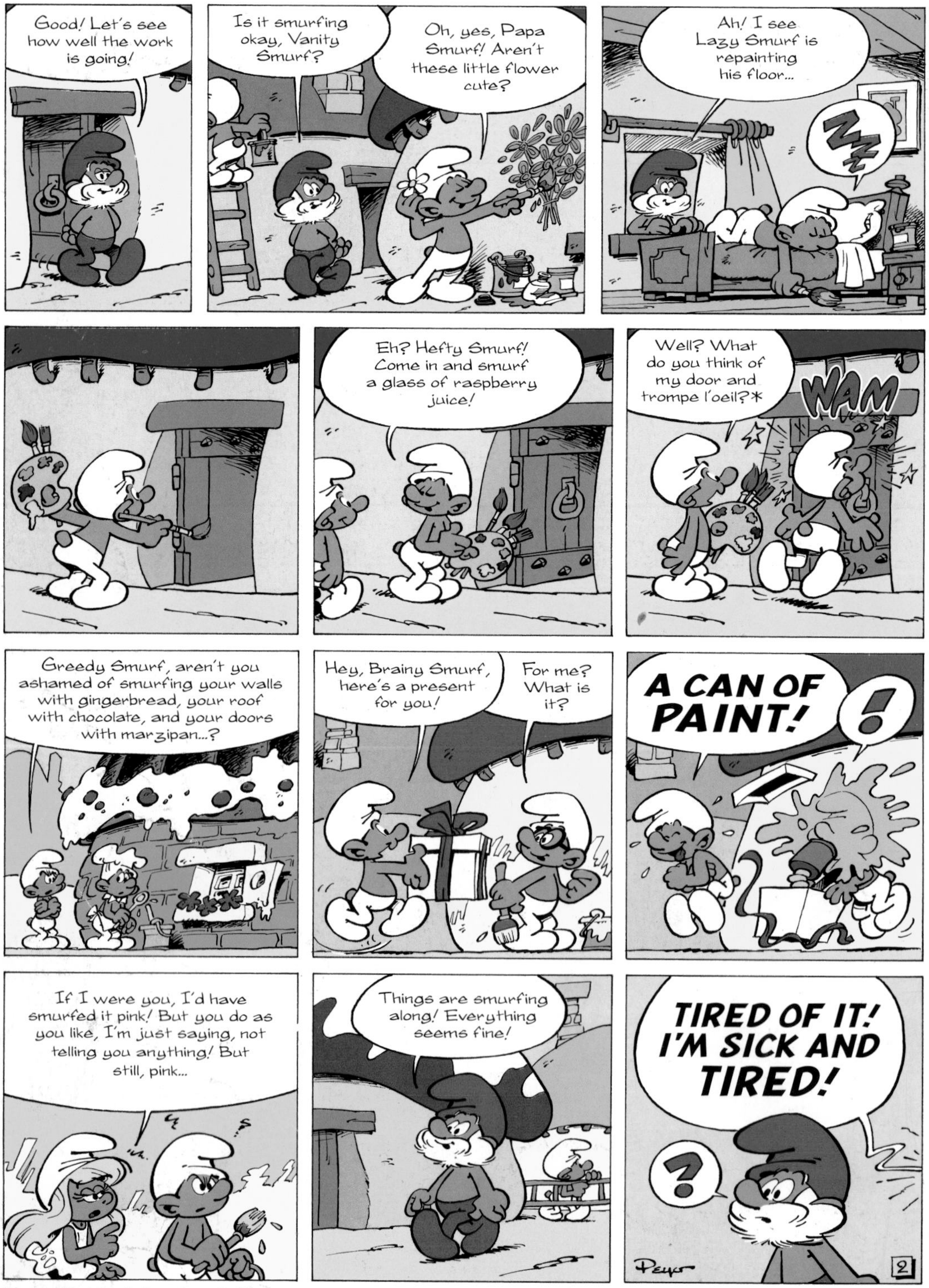
Good! Let's see how well the work is going!
Is it smurfing okay, Vanity Smurf?
Oh, yes, Papa Smurf! Aren't these little flower cute?
Ah! I see Lazy Smurf is repainting his floor...
ZZZ
Eh? Hefty Smurf! Come in and smurf a glass of raspberry juice!
Well? What do you think of my door and trompe l'oeil?*
WAM
Greedy Smurf, aren't you ashamed of smurfing your walls with gingerbread, your roof with chocolate, and your doors with marzipan...?
Hey, Brainy Smurf, here's a present for you!
For me? What is it?
A CAN OF PAINT!
!
If I were you, I'd have smurfed it pink! But you do as you like, I'm just saying, not telling you anything! But still, pink...
Things are smurfing along! Everything seems fine!
TIRED OF IT! I'M SICK AND TIRED!
?
2

*A style of painting that creates optical illusions.

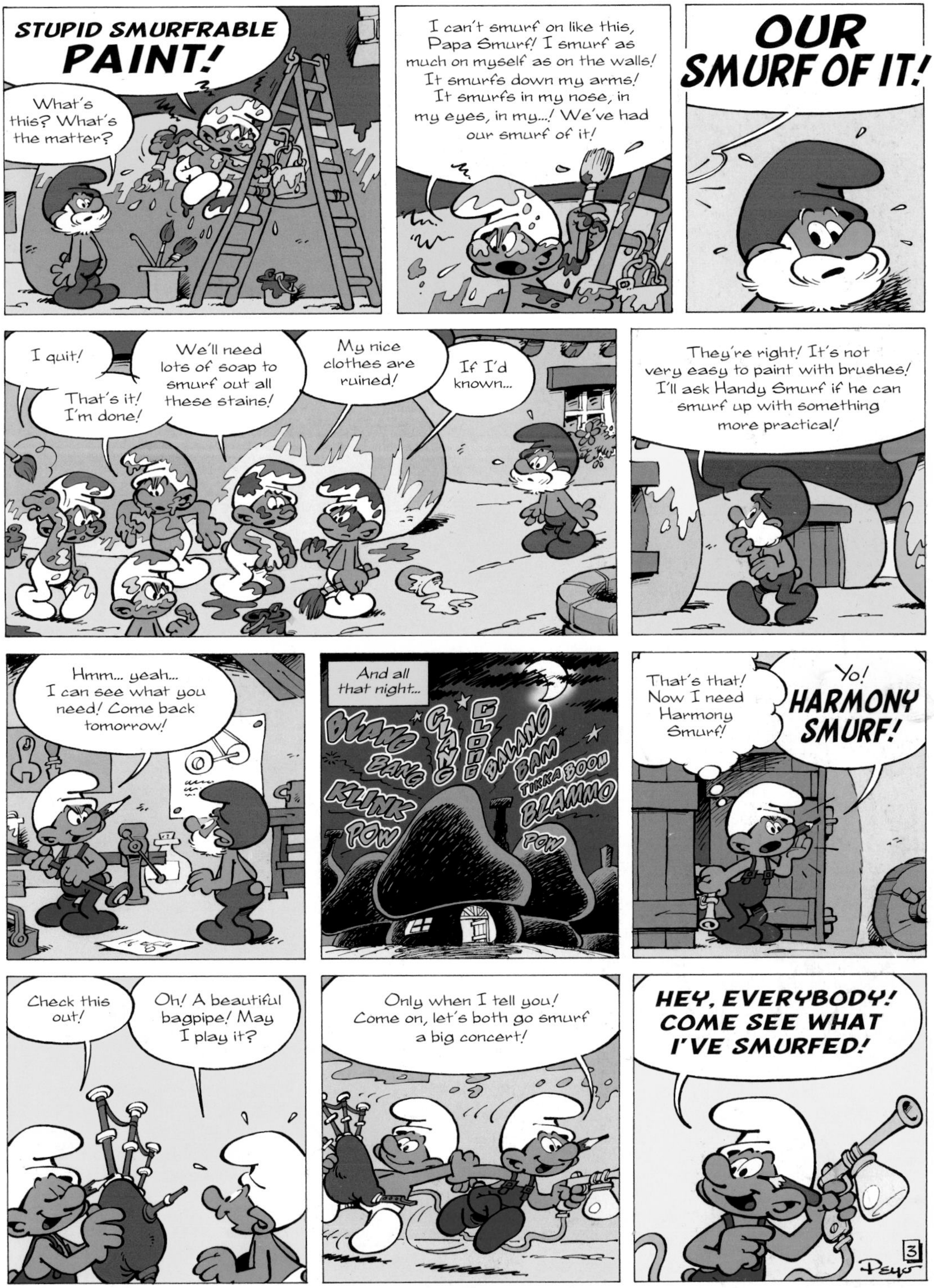
STUPID SMURFRABLE PAINT!
What's this? What's the matter?
I can't smurf on like this, Papa Smurf! I smurf as much on myself as on the walls! It smurfs down my arms! It smurfs in my nose, in my eyes, in my...! We've had our smurf of it!
OUR SMURF OF IT!
I quit!
That's it! I'm done!
We'll need lots of soap to smurf out all these stains!
My nice clothes are ruined!
If I'd known...
They're right! It's not very easy to paint with brushes! I'll ask Handy Smurf if he can smurf up with something more practical!
Hmm... yeah... I can see what you need! Come back tomorrow!
And all that night...
BLANG
BANG
CLANG
CLONG
BALANG
BAM
TIKKA BOOM
KLINK
POW
BLAMMO
POW
That's that! Now I need Harmony Smurf!
Yo! HARMONY SMURF!
Check this out!
Oh! A beautiful bagpipe! May I play it?
Only when I tell you! Come on, let's both go smurf a big concert!
HEY, EVERYBODY! COME SEE WHAT I'VE SMURFED!
3
Peyo

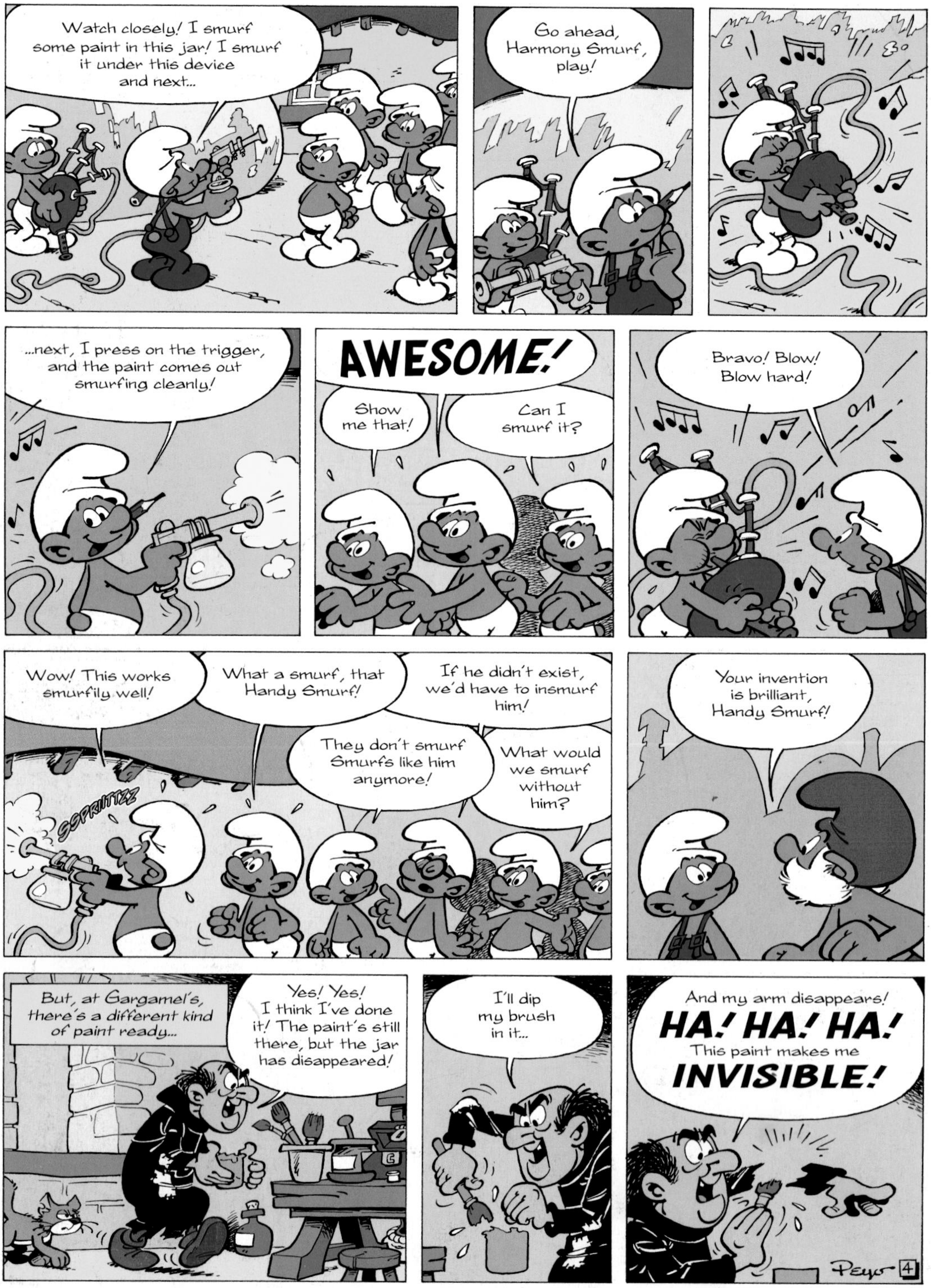
Watch closely! I smurf some paint in this jar! I smurf it under this device and next...
Go ahead, Harmony Smurf, play!
...next, I press on the trigger, and the paint comes out smurfing cleanly!
AWESOME!
Show me that!
Can I smurf it?
Bravo! Blow! Blow hard!
Wow! This works smurfily well!
What a smurf, that Handy Smurf!
If he didn't exist, we'd have to insmurf him!
They don't smurf Smurfs like him anymore!
What would we smurf without him?
SSPRIITTZZ
Your invention is brilliant, Handy Smurf!
But, at Gargamel's, there's a different kind of paint ready...
Yes! Yes! I think I've done it! The paint's still there, but the jar has disappeared!
I'll dip my brush in it...
And my arm disappears! HA! HA! HA! This paint makes me INVISIBLE!
Peyo
4

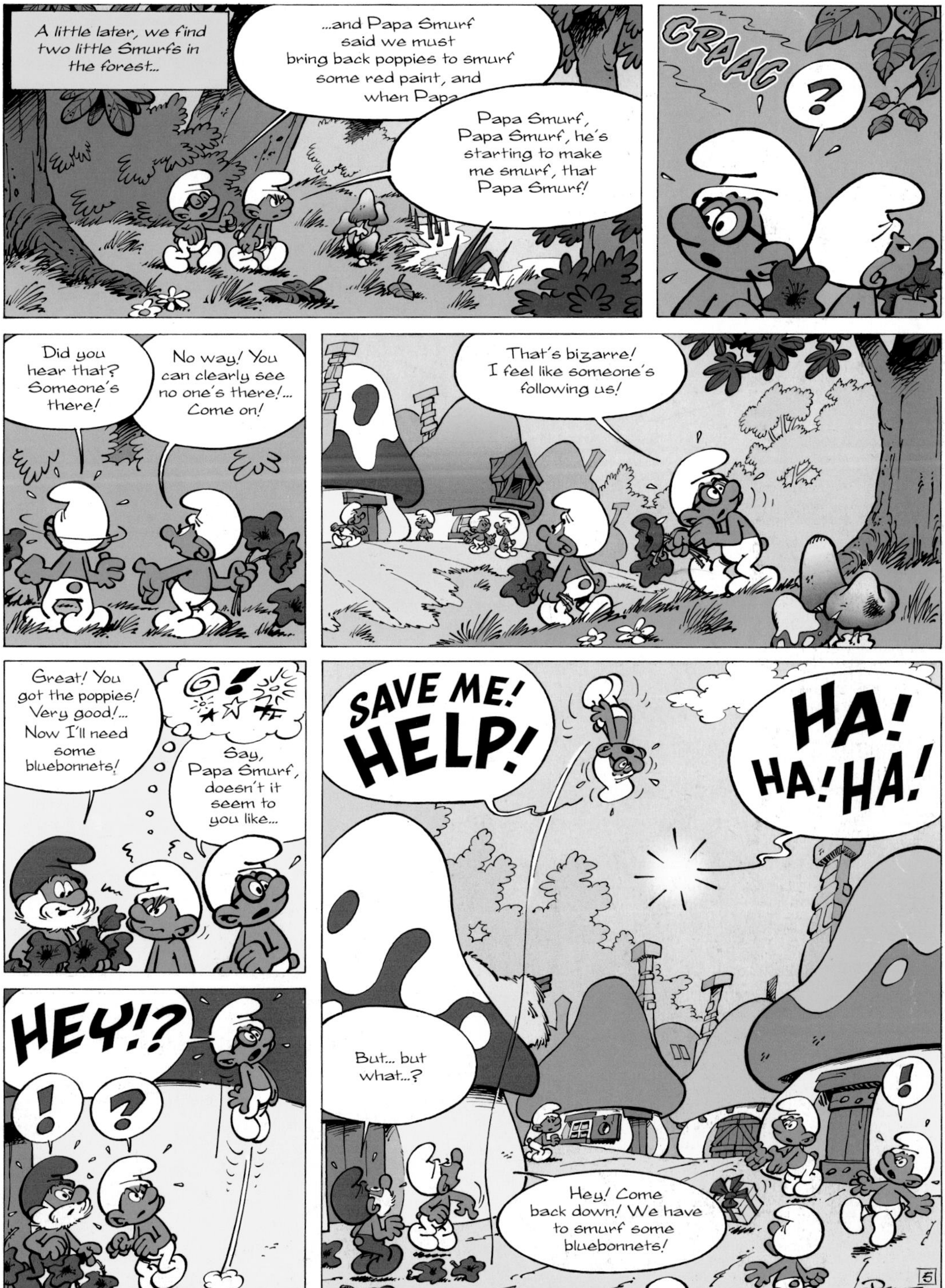
A little later, we find two little Smurfs in the forest...
...and Papa Smurf said we must bring back poppies to smurf some red paint, and when Papa
Papa Smurf, Papa Smurf, he's starting to make me smurf, that Papa Smurf!
CRAAC
?
Did you hear that? Someone's there!
No way! You can clearly see no one's there!... Come on!
That's bizarre! I feel like someone's following us!
Great! You got the poppies! Very good!... Now I'll need some bluebonnets!
Say, Papa Smurf, doesn't it seem to you like...
HEY!?
!
?
SAVE ME! HELP!
HA! HA! HA!
But... but what...?
Hey! Come back down! We have to smurf some bluebonnets!
!
5
PEYO

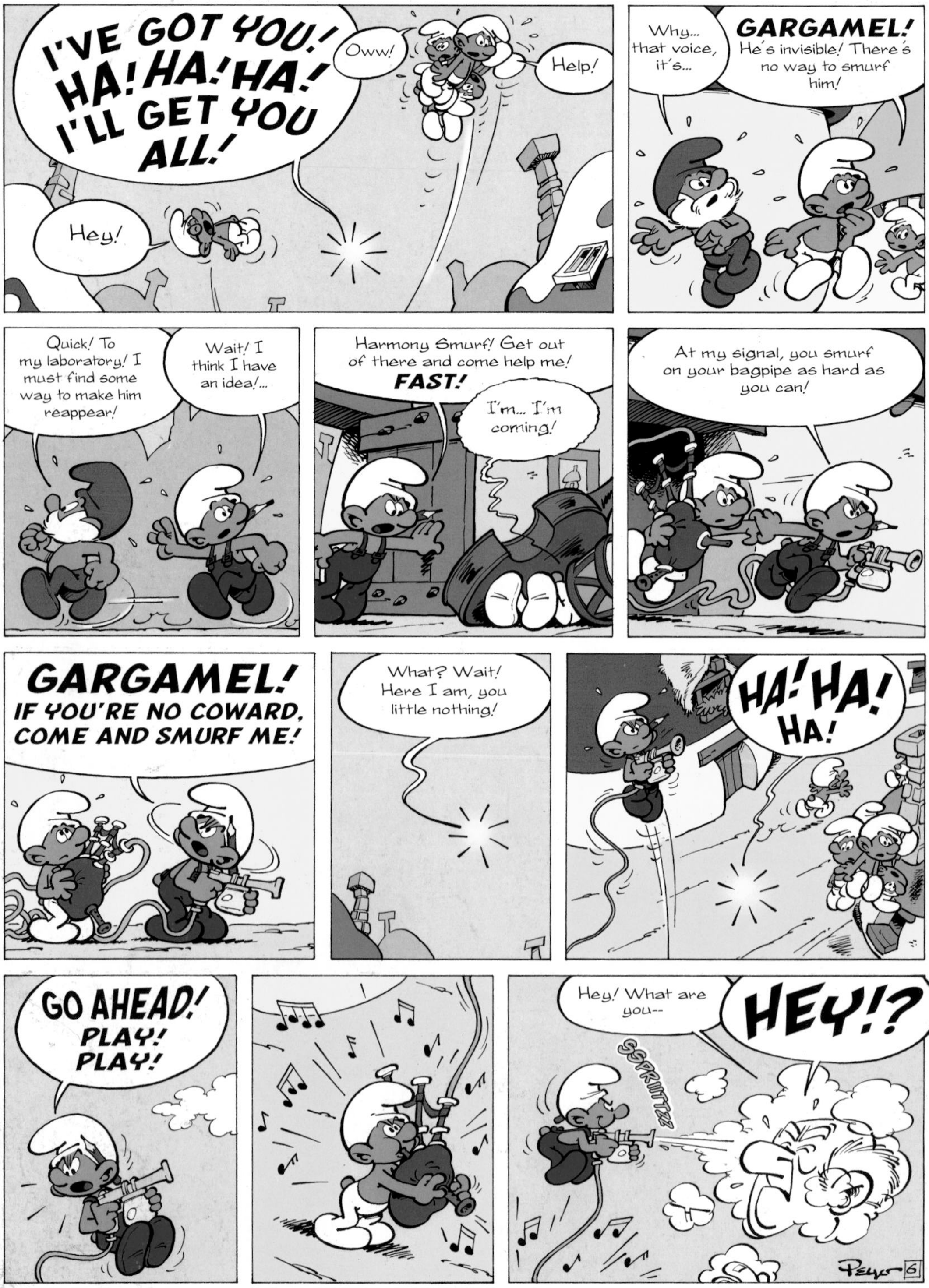
I'VE GOT YOU! HA! HA! HA! I'LL GET YOU ALL!
Oww!
Help!
Hey!
Why... that voice, it's...
GARGAMEL! He's invisible! There's no way to smurf him!
Quick! To my laboratory! I must find some way to make him reappear!
Wait! I think I have an idea!...
Harmony Smurf! Get out of there and come help me! FAST!
I'm... I'm coming!
At my signal, you smurf on your bagpipe as hard as you can!
GARGAMEL! IF YOU'RE NO COWARD, COME AND SMURF ME!
What? Wait! Here I am, you little nothing!
HA! HA! HA!
GO AHEAD! PLAY! PLAY!
Hey! What are you--
HEY!?
SSPRIIITZZZ
Peyo
6

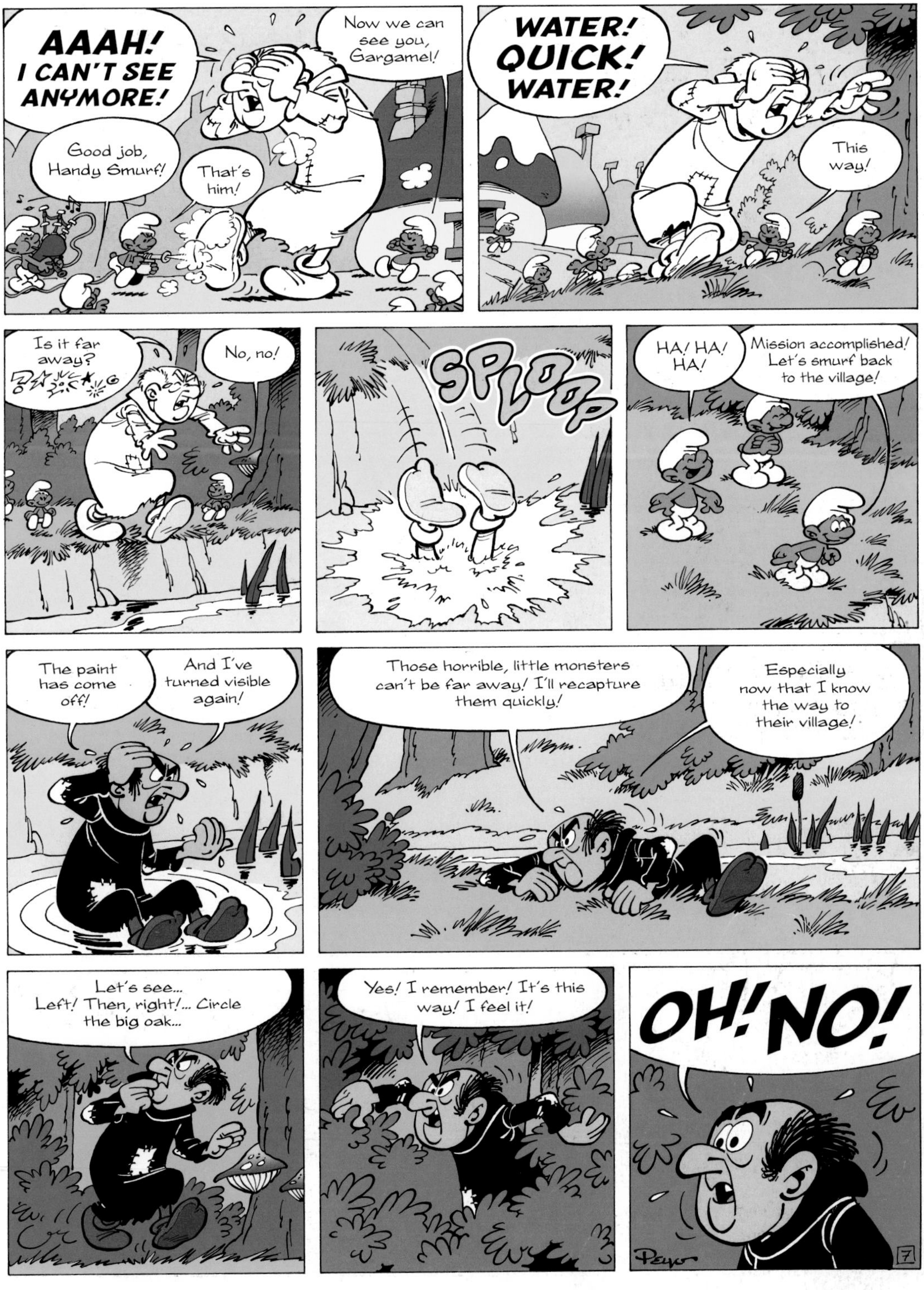
AAAH! I CAN'T SEE ANYMORE!
Now we can see you, Gargamel!
Good job, Handy Smurf!
That's him!
WATER! QUICK! WATER!
This way!
Is it far away?
No, no!
SPLOOP
HA! HA! HA!
Mission accomplished! Let's smurf back to the village!
The paint has come off!
And I've turned visible again!
Those horrible, little monsters can't be far away! I'll recapture them quickly!
Especially now that I know the way to their village!
Let's see... Left! Then, right!... Circle the big oak...
Yes! I remember! It's this way! I feel it!
OH! NO!
Peyo
7

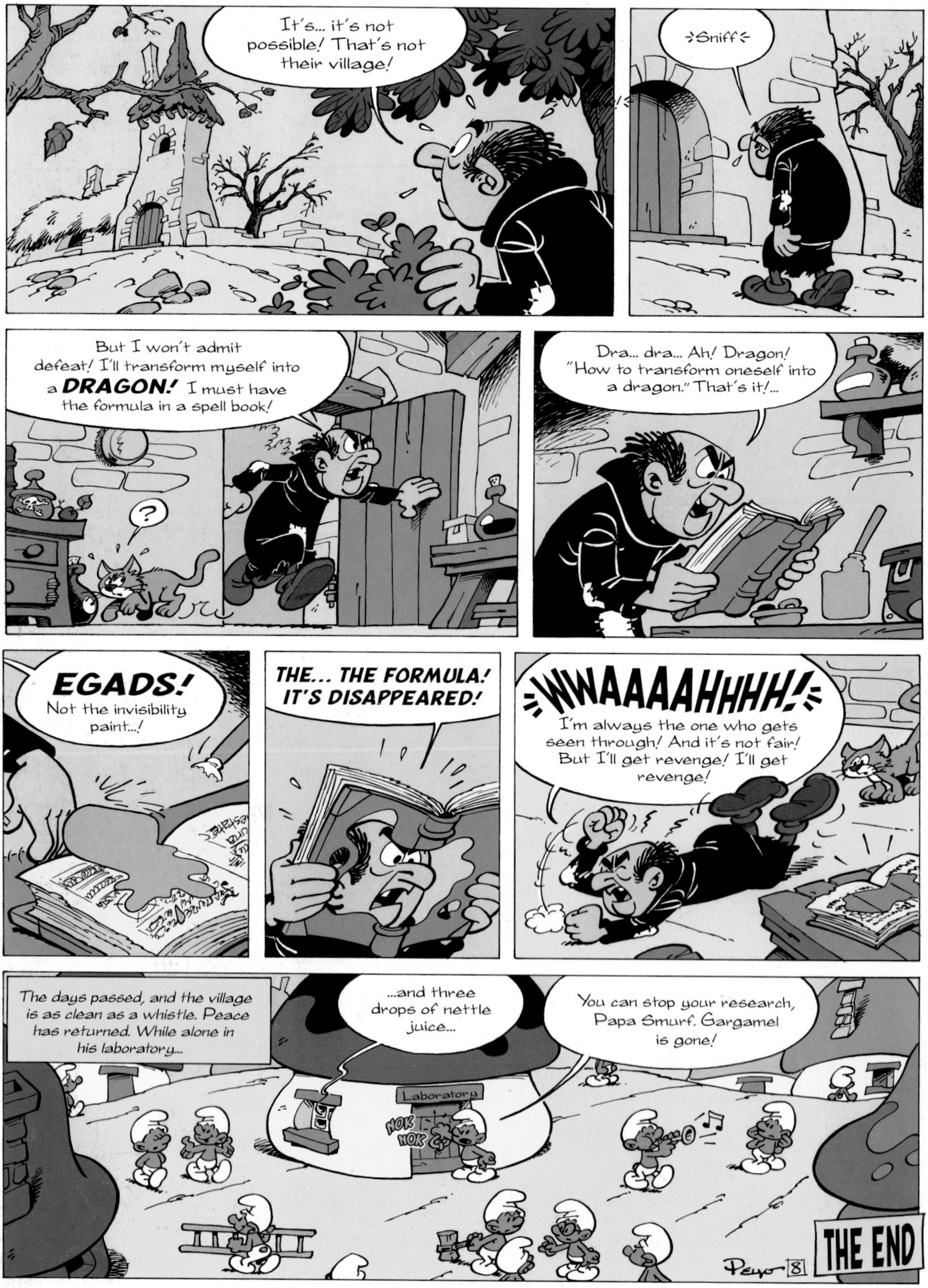

It's... it's not possible! That's not their village!
Sniff
But I won't admit defeat! I'll transform myself into a **DRAGON!** I must have the formula in a spell book!
?
Dra... dra... Ah! Dragon! "How to transform oneself into a dragon." That's it!...
EGADS! Not the invisibility paint...!
THE... THE FORMULA! IT'S DISAPPEARED!
WWAAAAAHHHH! I'm always the one who gets seen through! And it's not fair! But I'll get revenge! I'll get revenge!
The days passed, and the village is as clean as a whistle. Peace has returned. While alone in his laboratory...
...and three drops of nettle juice...
You can stop your research, Papa Smurf. Gargamel is gone!
Laboratory
NOK NOK
THE END
Peyo 8

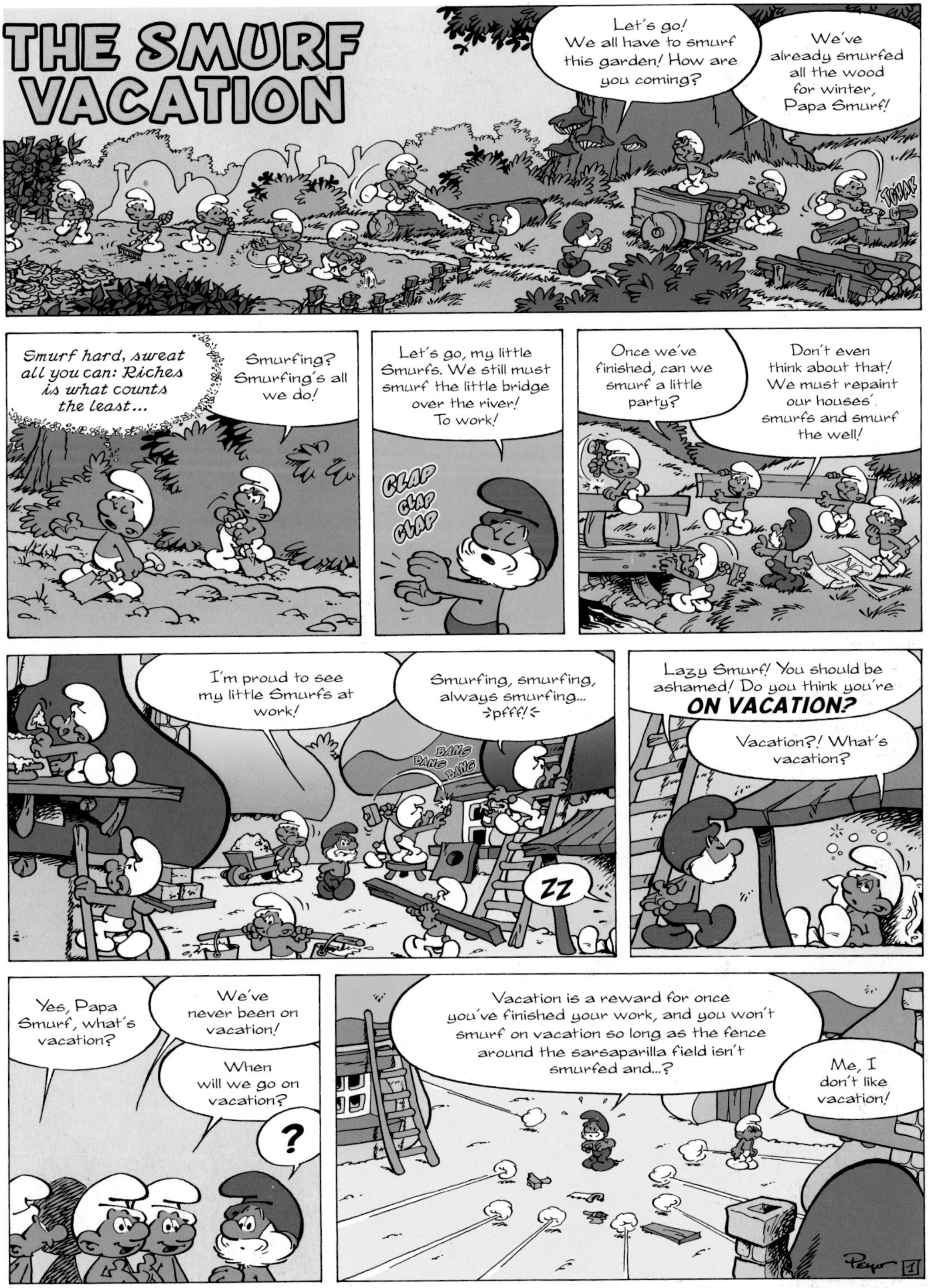
THE SMURF VACATION
Let's go! We all have to smurf this garden! How are you coming?
We've already smurfed all the wood for winter, Papa Smurf!
Smurf hard, sweat all you can: Riches is what counts the least...
Smurfing? Smurfing's all we do!
Let's go, my little Smurfs. We still must smurf the little bridge over the river! To work!
CLAP CLAP CLAP
Once we've finished, can we smurf a little party?
Don't even think about that! We must repaint our houses' smurfs and smurf the well!
I'm proud to see my little Smurfs at work!
Smurfing, smurfing, always smurfing... >pfff!<
BANG BANG BANG
ZZ
Lazy Smurf! You should be ashamed! Do you think you're ON VACATION?
Vacation?! What's vacation?
Yes, Papa Smurf, what's vacation?
We've never been on vacation!
When will we go on vacation?
?
Vacation is a reward for once you've finished your work, and you won't smurf on vacation so long as the fence around the sarsaparilla field isn't smurfed and...?
Me, I don't like vacation!
Peyo
1

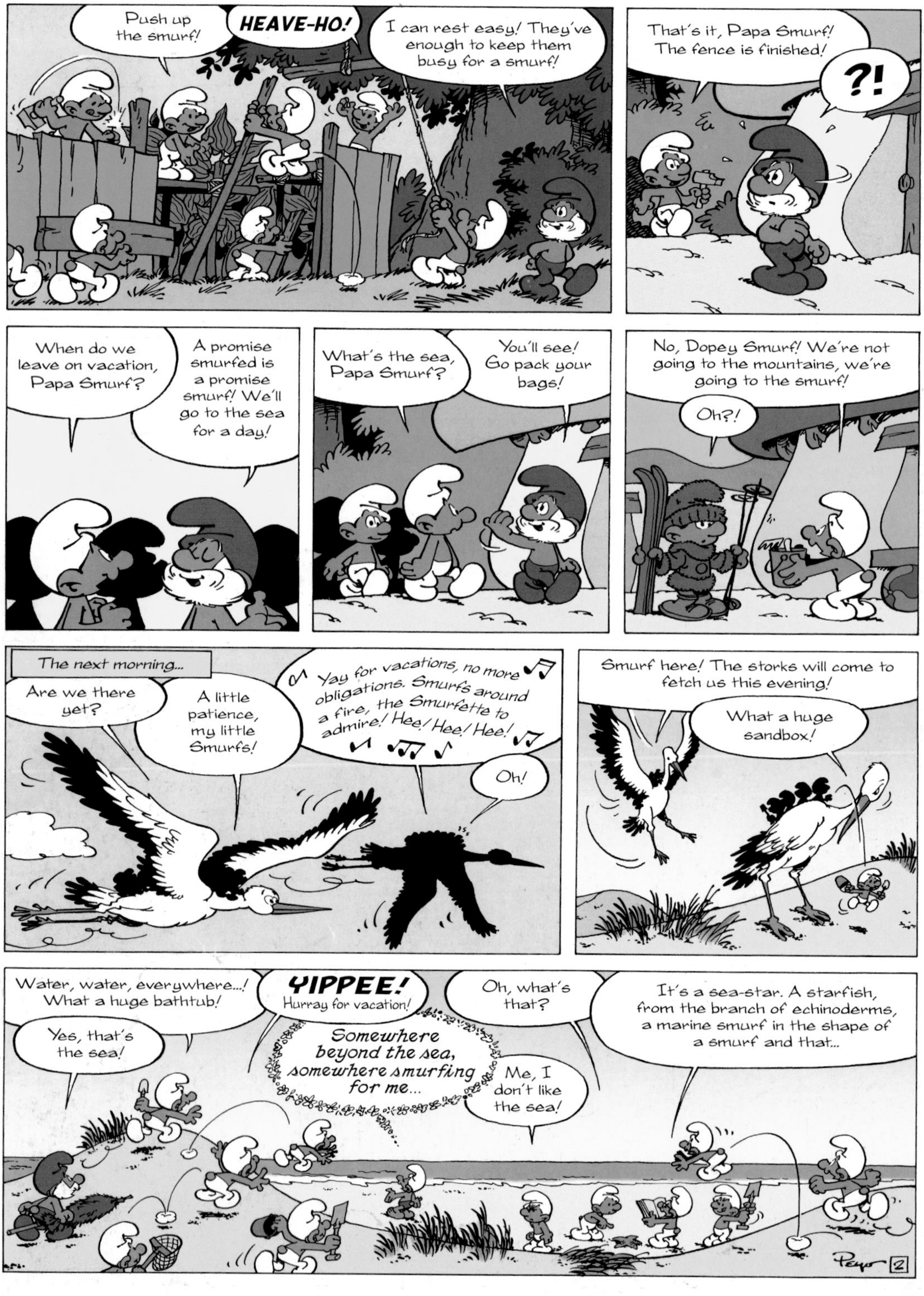
Push up the smurf!
HEAVE-HO!
I can rest easy! They've enough to keep them busy for a smurf!
That's it, Papa Smurf! The fence is finished!
?!
When do we leave on vacation, Papa Smurf?
A promise smurfed is a promise smurf! We'll go to the sea for a day!
What's the sea, Papa Smurf?
You'll see! Go pack your bags!
No, Dopey Smurf! We're not going to the mountains, we're going to the smurf!
Oh?!
The next morning...
Are we there yet?
A little patience, my little Smurfs!
Yay for vacations, no more obligations. Smurfs around a fire, the Smurfette to admire! Hee! Hee! Hee!
Oh!
Smurf here! The storks will come to fetch us this evening!
What a huge sandbox!
Water, water, everywhere...! What a huge bathtub!
Yes, that's the sea!
YIPPEE! Hurray for vacation!
Somewhere beyond the sea, somewhere smurfing for me...
Oh, what's that?
Me, I don't like the sea!
It's a sea-star. A starfish, from the branch of echinoderms, a marine smurf in the shape of a smurf and that...
Peyo
2

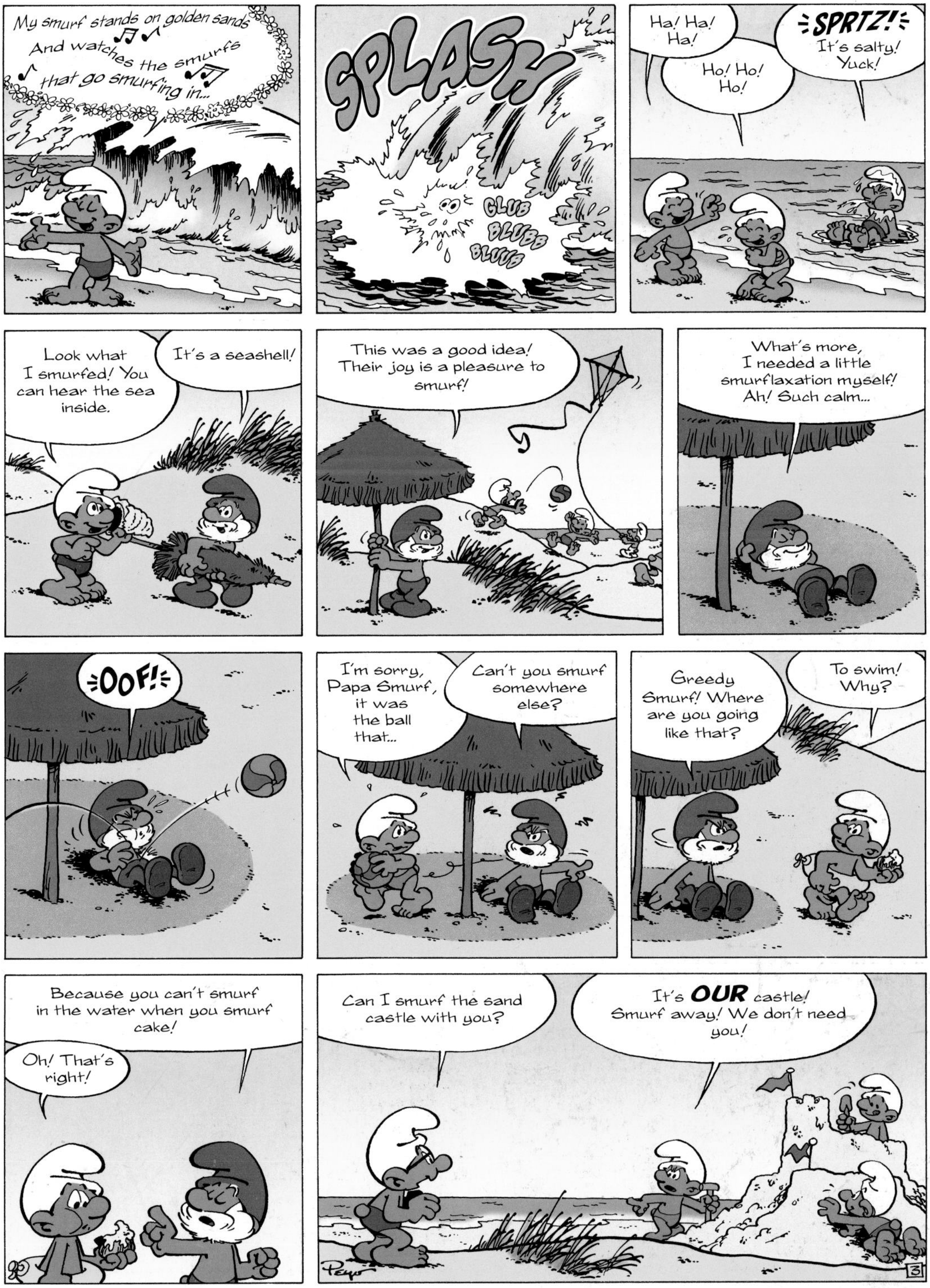
My smurf stands on golden sands
And watches the smurfs
that go smurfing in...
SPLASH
GLUB
BLUBB
BLUUB
Ha! Ha! Ha!
Ho! Ho! Ho!
SPRTZ!
It's salty! Yuck!
Look what I smurfed! You can hear the sea inside.
It's a seashell!
This was a good idea! Their joy is a pleasure to smurf!
What's more, I needed a little smurflaxation myself! Ah! Such calm...
OOF!
I'm sorry, Papa Smurf, it was the ball that...
Can't you smurf somewhere else?
Greedy Smurf! Where are you going like that?
To swim! Why?
Because you can't smurf in the water when you smurf cake!
Oh! That's right!
Can I smurf the sand castle with you?
It's OUR castle! Smurf away! We don't need you!
Peyo
3

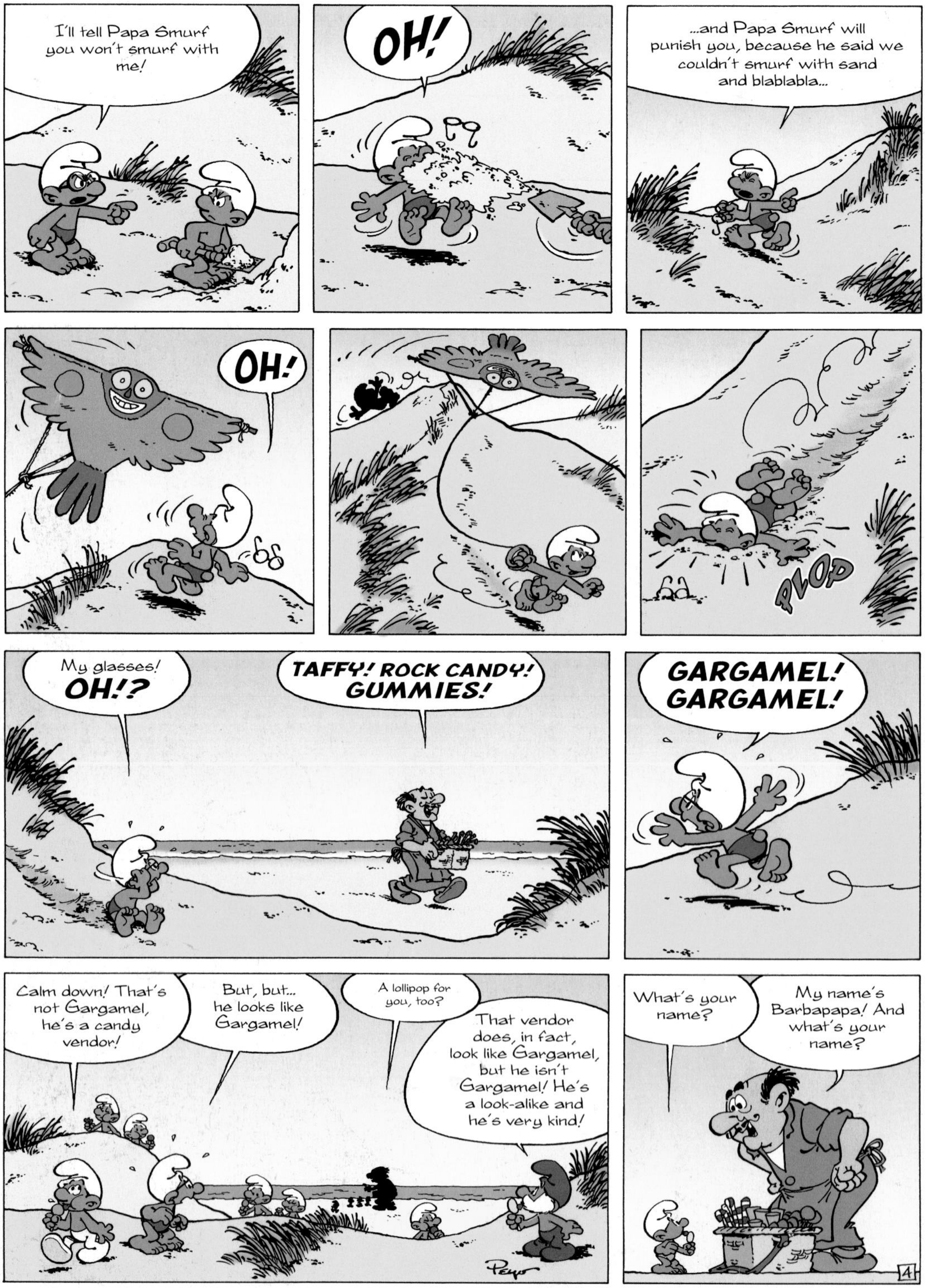
I'll tell Papa Smurf you won't smurf with me!
OH!
...and Papa Smurf will punish you, because he said we couldn't smurf with sand and blablabla...
OH!
PLOP
My glasses! OH!?
TAFFY! ROCK CANDY! GUMMIES!
GARGAMEL! GARGAMEL!
Calm down! That's not Gargamel, he's a candy vendor!
But, but... he looks like Gargamel!
A lollipop for you, too?
That vendor does, in fact, look like Gargamel, but he isn't Gargamel! He's a look-alike and he's very kind!
What's your name?
My name's Barbapapa! And what's your name?
4

Well, my name is Smurf! We're all Smurfs!

Smurf, that's a pretty name for an elf!

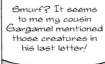

Smurf? It seems to me my cousin Gargamel mentioned those creatures in his last letter!

Here's Gargamel's letter...

"...If one day you meet the Smurfs, capture them and let me know! They're horrible vermin!"

Bah, Gargamel always exaggerates. Those Smurfs seem very nice and, after all, a customer's a customer!

Barbapapa, can I smurf another lollipop?

You owe me a quarter for the one you already ate. That'll be two quarters!

But I don't have any money. Finance Smurf said we mustn't smurf anymore with money! (*)

What do you mean, no money?

Are you saying you refuse to pay me?

For what?

My cousin Gargamel's right: these Smurfs **ARE** horrible vermin! I'm going to follow his letter's recommendations!

How can I trap them with no risk? They could be dangerous!

Ohooh! Those old hives give me an idea! Just need a few modifications...

Done! There's a lock on each door. Now, I have to lure them inside these little cabins.

Everybody in the water, it's time!

Wait, I'm taking off my smurf!

*See THE SMURFS #18 "The Finance Smurf."

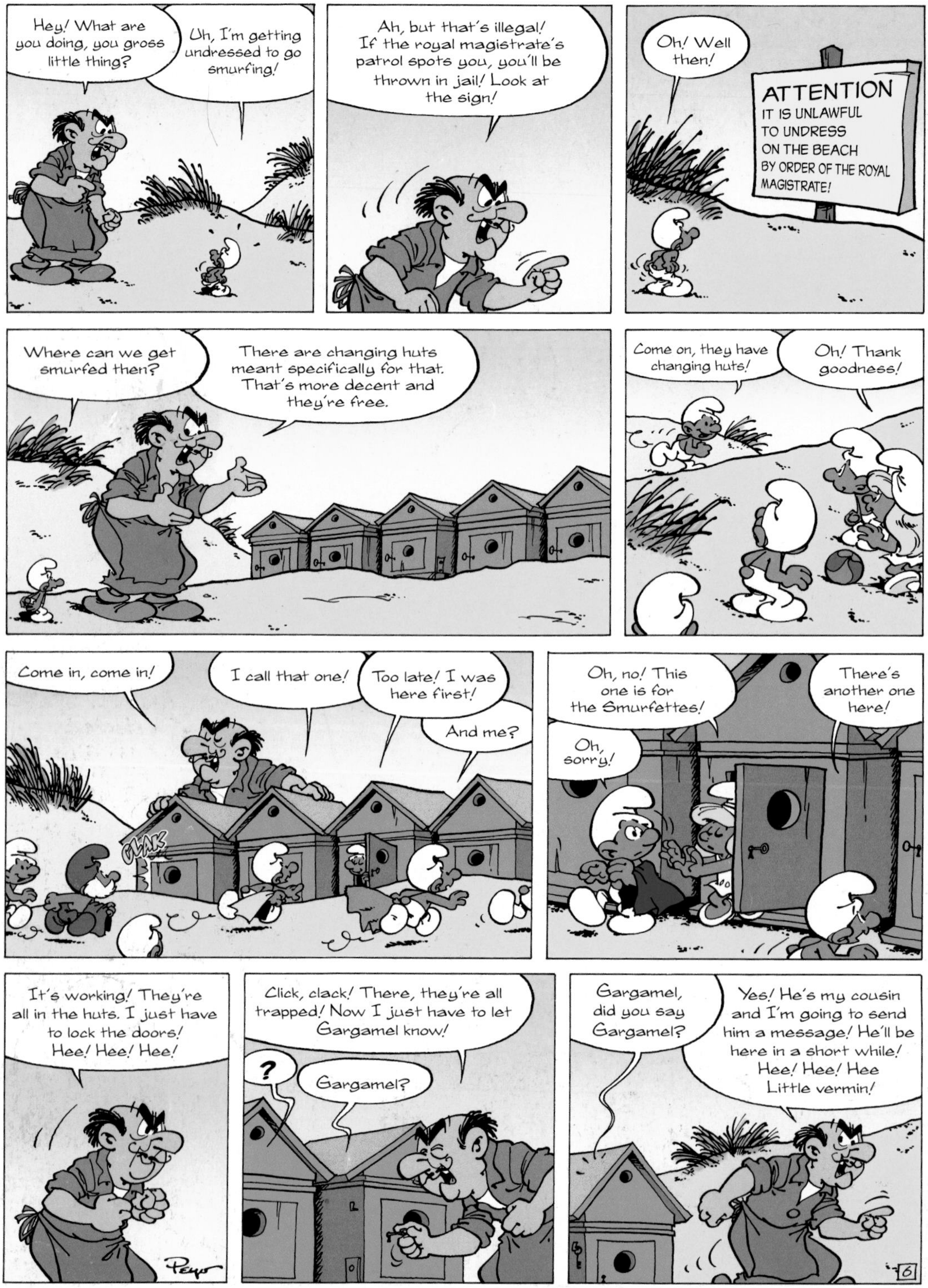
Hey! What are you doing, you gross little thing?
Uh, I'm getting undressed to go smurfing!
Ah, but that's illegal! If the royal magistrate's patrol spots you, you'll be thrown in jail! Look at the sign!
Oh! Well then!
ATTENTION IT IS UNLAWFUL TO UNDRESS ON THE BEACH BY ORDER OF THE ROYAL MAGISTRATE!
Where can we get smurfed then?
There are changing huts meant specifically for that. That's more decent and they're free.
Come on, they have changing huts!
Oh! Thank goodness!
Come in, come in!
I call that one!
Too late! I was here first!
And me?
CLAK
Oh, no! This one is for the Smurfettes!
Oh, sorry!
There's another one here!
It's working! They're all in the huts. I just have to lock the doors! Hee! Hee! Hee!
Peyo
Click, clack! There, they're all trapped! Now I just have to let Gargamel know!
?
Gargamel?
Gargamel, did you say Gargamel?
Yes! He's my cousin and I'm going to send him a message! He'll be here in a short while! Hee! Hee! Hee Little vermin!
6

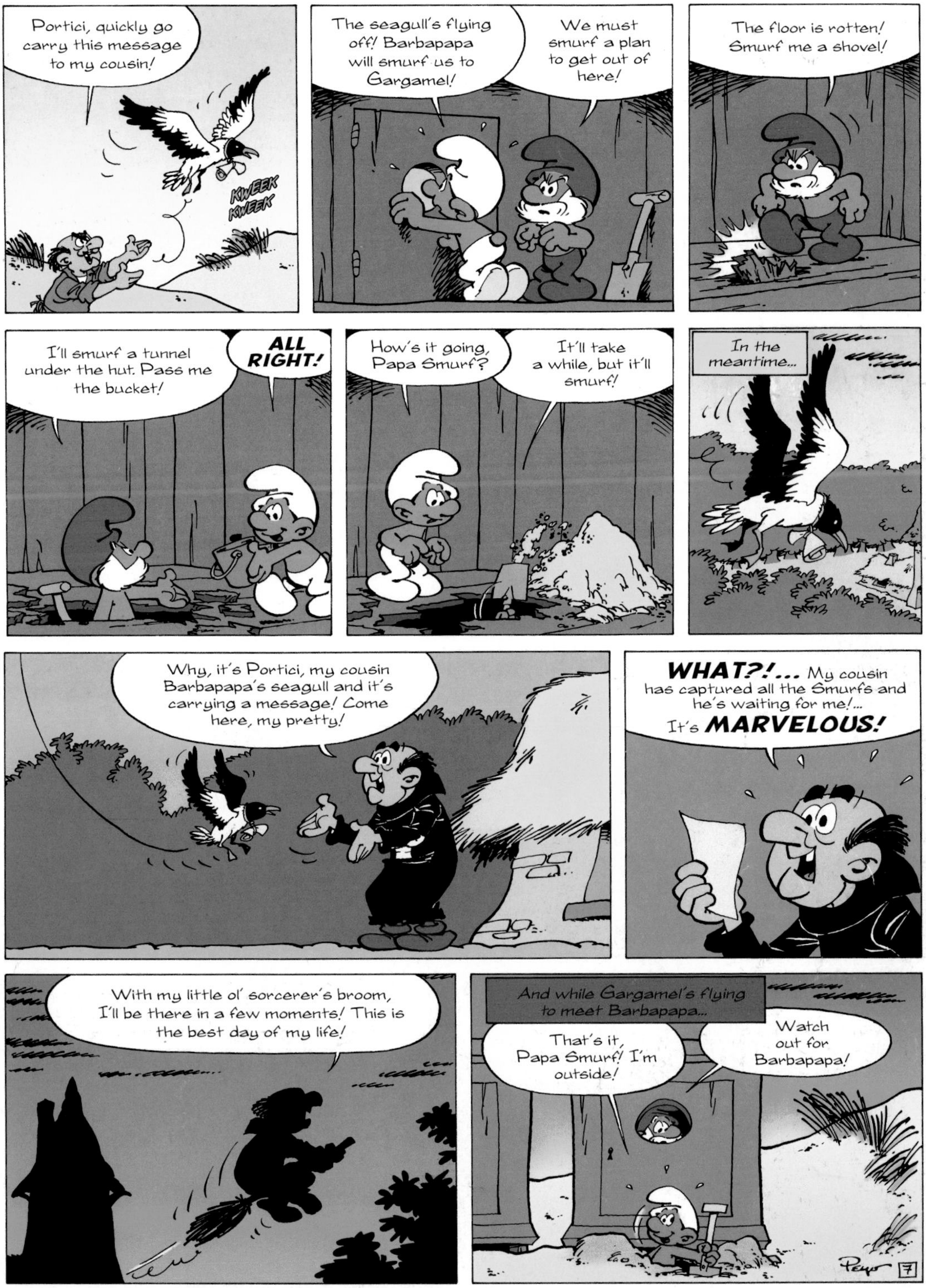

Portici, quickly go carry this message to my cousin!
KWEEK KWEEK
The seagull's flying off! Barbapapa will smurf us to Gargamel!
We must smurf a plan to get out of here!
The floor is rotten! Smurf me a shovel!
I'll smurf a tunnel under the hut. Pass me the bucket!
ALL RIGHT!
How's it going, Papa Smurf?
It'll take a while, but it'll smurf!
In the meantime...
Why, it's Portici, my cousin Barbapapa's seagull and it's carrying a message! Come here, my pretty!
WHAT?!... My cousin has captured all the Smurfs and he's waiting for me!... It's MARVELOUS!
With my little ol' sorcerer's broom, I'll be there in a few moments! This is the best day of my life!
And while Gargamel's flying to meet Barbapapa...
That's it, Papa Smurf! I'm outside!
Watch out for Barbapapa!
Peyo
7

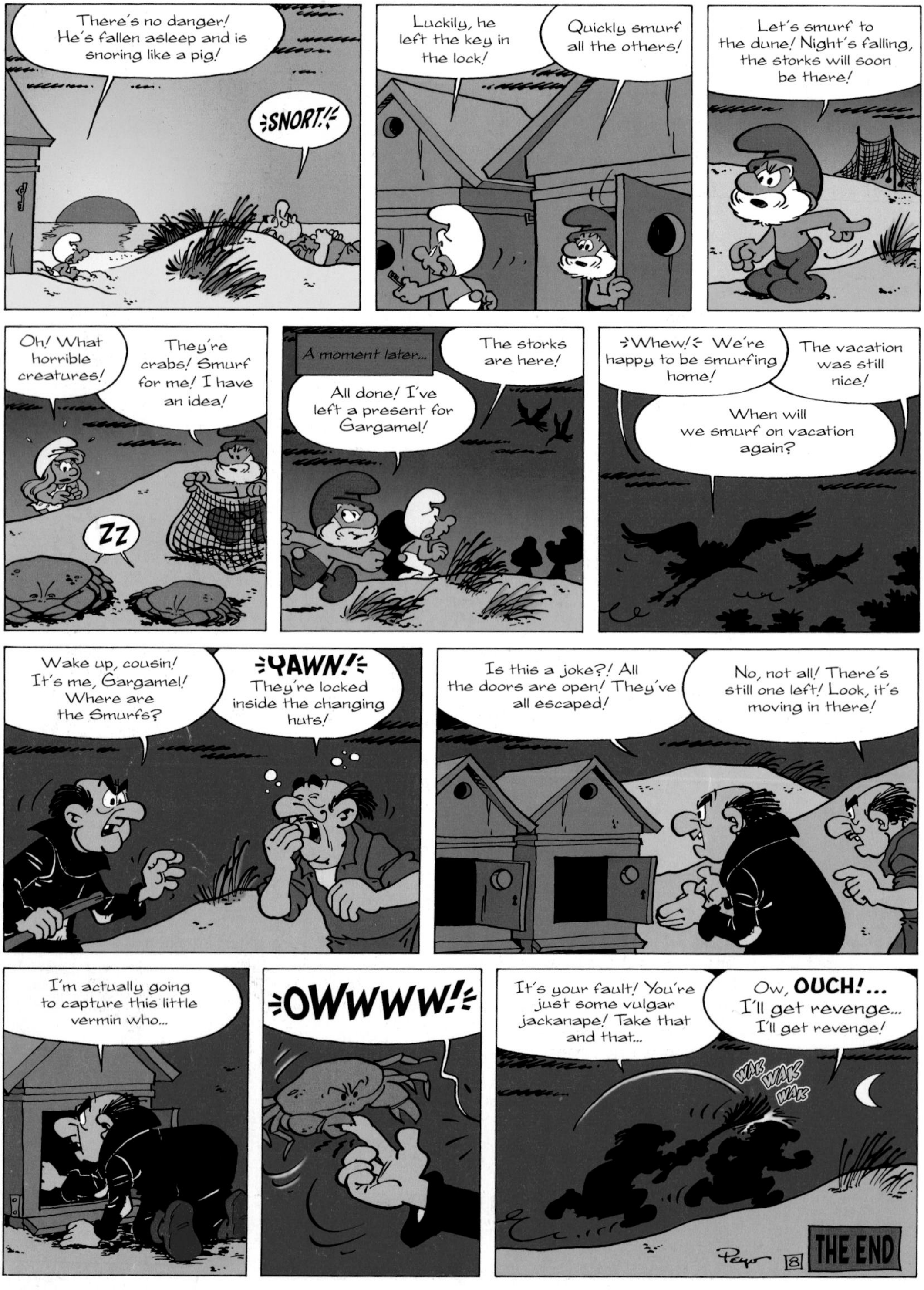
There's no danger! He's fallen asleep and is snoring like a pig!
SNORT!
Luckily, he left the key in the lock!
Quickly smurf all the others!
Let's smurf to the dune! Night's falling, the storks will soon be there!
Oh! What horrible creatures!
They're crabs! Smurf for me! I have an idea!
ZZ
A moment later...
The storks are here!
All done! I've left a present for Gargamel!
Whew! We're happy to be smurfing home!
The vacation was still nice!
When will we smurf on vacation again?
Wake up, cousin! It's me, Gargamel! Where are the Smurfs?
YAWN! They're locked inside the changing huts!
Is this a joke?! All the doors are open! They've all escaped!
No, not all! There's still one left! Look, it's moving in there!
I'm actually going to capture this little vermin who...
OWWWW!
It's your fault! You're just some vulgar jackanape! Take that and that...
Ow, OUCH!... I'll get revenge... I'll get revenge!
WAK WAK WAK
Peyo
8
THE END

# WATCH OUT FOR PAPERCUTZ™

Welcome to the tempestuously talkative twelfth SMURFS graphic novel by Peyo (and Yvan Delporte) from Papercutz, the plain-speaking publisher of great graphic novels for all ages. I'm Jim Salicrup, your Yankee-accented Smurf-in-Chief.

As all Smurf scholars already know, the battle over how to speak the Smurf language properly in "Smurf Vs. Smurf" is inspired by the ongoing dispute between the Dutch- and French-speaking communities in the authors' native country of Belgium. It also demonstrates how "human" the Smurfs can act at times. I personally believe that communication is one of the most difficult things we all do. We're all very emotional creatures, and it's often very easy to misinterpret what someone really means. I also believe, that if you took the two nicest people on Earth (pick any two!) and locked them into the same room for a month—they'd eventually be at each other's throats!

Don't get me wrong (he writes, without any sense of irony), I do believe in Peace and Love, and I'm very optimistic about the fate of mankind, but it just seems that it can be very difficult for humans to actually get along at times. Just look at how folks tend to act during an election year. Everyone gets very passionate about their candidate or political party or a particular pet issue. Constructive and meaningful debate is certainly a good thing, but when people decide that they're right, and you're wrong, things can get out of hand and become needlessly hurtful and counterproductive. You know, it's not a bad idea for all of us (especially me!) to try to be a little more respectful of others' opinions and views, and try to do our best to see the other person's side—even when we don't agree.

That's enough sermonizing (or Smurfonizing)! The big news for all the super-serious Smurf-completists out there is that the second FREE COMIC BOOK DAY comic from Papercutz was released earlier this year. FREE COMIC BOOK DAY may be my absolute favorite unofficial holiday. It's usually the first Saturday in May, and it's when participating comicbook stores all across North America actually give away special FREE COMIC BOOK DAY comics published by all the top comicbook and graphic novel publishers.

Last year, the very first FREE COMIC BOOK DAY comic from Papercutz was published and it featured a great big preview of a GERONIMO STILTON graphic novel, as well as a complete SMURFS story, and several Smurfs comic strips. For the 2012 edition, we've gone all out and are featuring the complete Smurfs story, "The Smurfs and the Booglooboo," in which our little blue buddies encounter a somewhat more benign Howlibird-type. The story spotlights Brainy Smurf and the Smurfette, and of course, features the villainy of Gargamel. There's also sequences from ERNEST & REBECCA #1 "My Best Friend is a Germ," which tells how 6 ½ year-old Rebecca met the microbial Ernest; and DANCE CLASS #1 "So, You Think You Can Hip-Hop?" which introduces us to Julie, Alia, Lucie, and few others from the DANCE CLASS crew!

And the DISNEY FAIRIES star in two all-new, complete stories—"Tinker Bell and the Forces of Nature" and "Express Yourself... Pixie Style." If you love stories about folks who live in a faraway land, in a small community, with danger always lurking nearby, then you'll love DISNEY FAIRIES! !

Of course, if you enjoyed *this* SMURFS graphic novel, you'll love SMURFS #13, "Smurf Soup" coming soon.

FREE COMIC BOOK DAY
PAPERCUTZ
the SMURFS
Peyo
PLUS: DISNEY FAIRIES, DANCE CLASS AND ERNEST & REBECCA
PAPERCUTZ


Smurf you later,

Jim

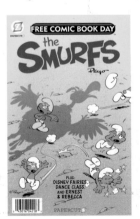

# EASTER SMURFS

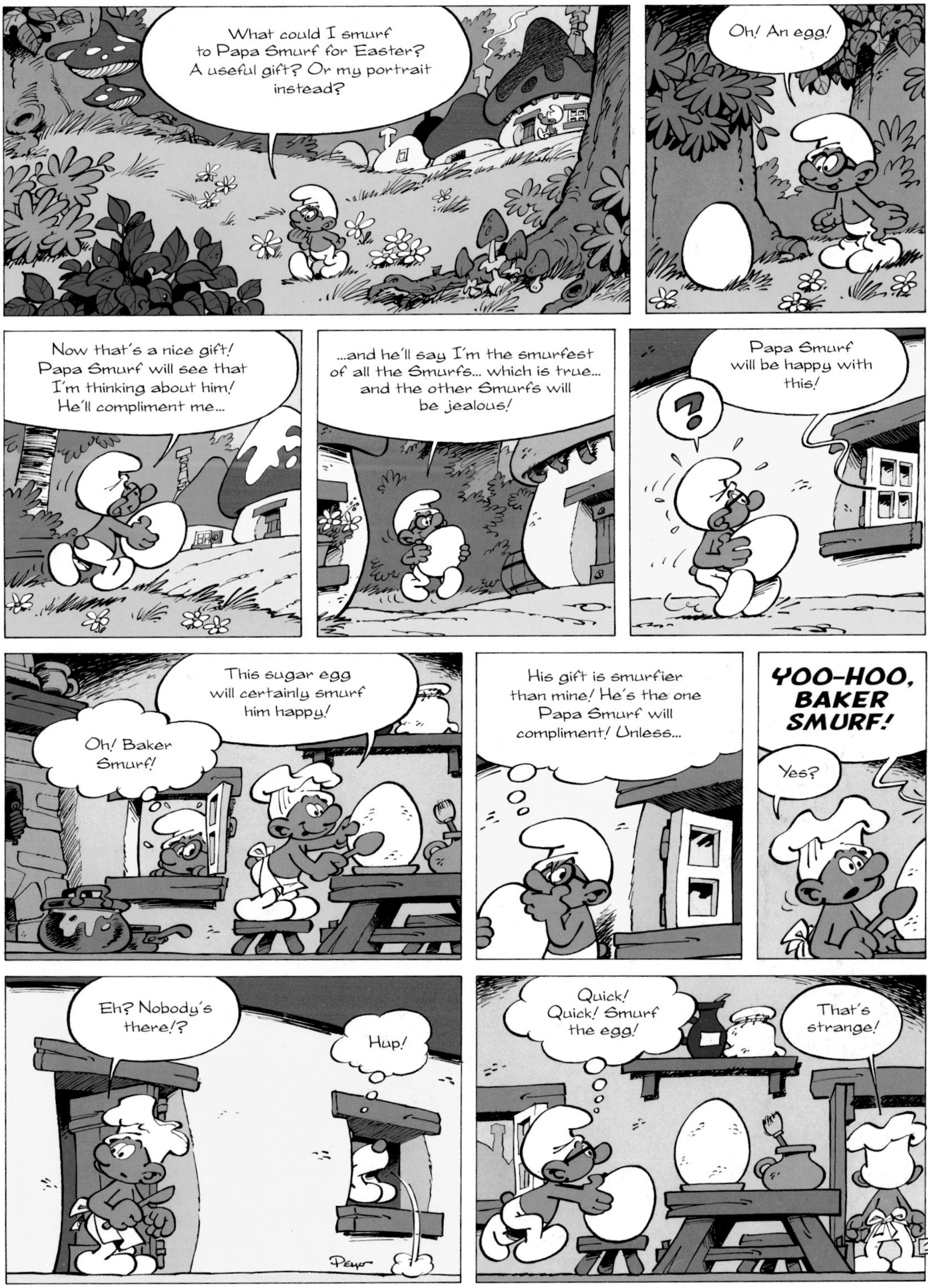
What could I smurf to Papa Smurf for Easter? A useful gift? Or my portrait instead?
Oh! An egg!
Now that's a nice gift! Papa Smurf will see that I'm thinking about him! He'll compliment me...
...and he'll say I'm the smurfest of all the Smurfs... which is true... and the other Smurfs will be jealous!
Papa Smurf will be happy with this!
?
This sugar egg will certainly smurf him happy!
Oh! Baker Smurf!
His gift is smurfier than mine! He's the one Papa Smurf will compliment! Unless...
YOO-HOO, BAKER SMURF!
Yes?
Eh? Nobody's there!?
Hup!
Quick! Quick! Smurf the egg!
That's strange!
1

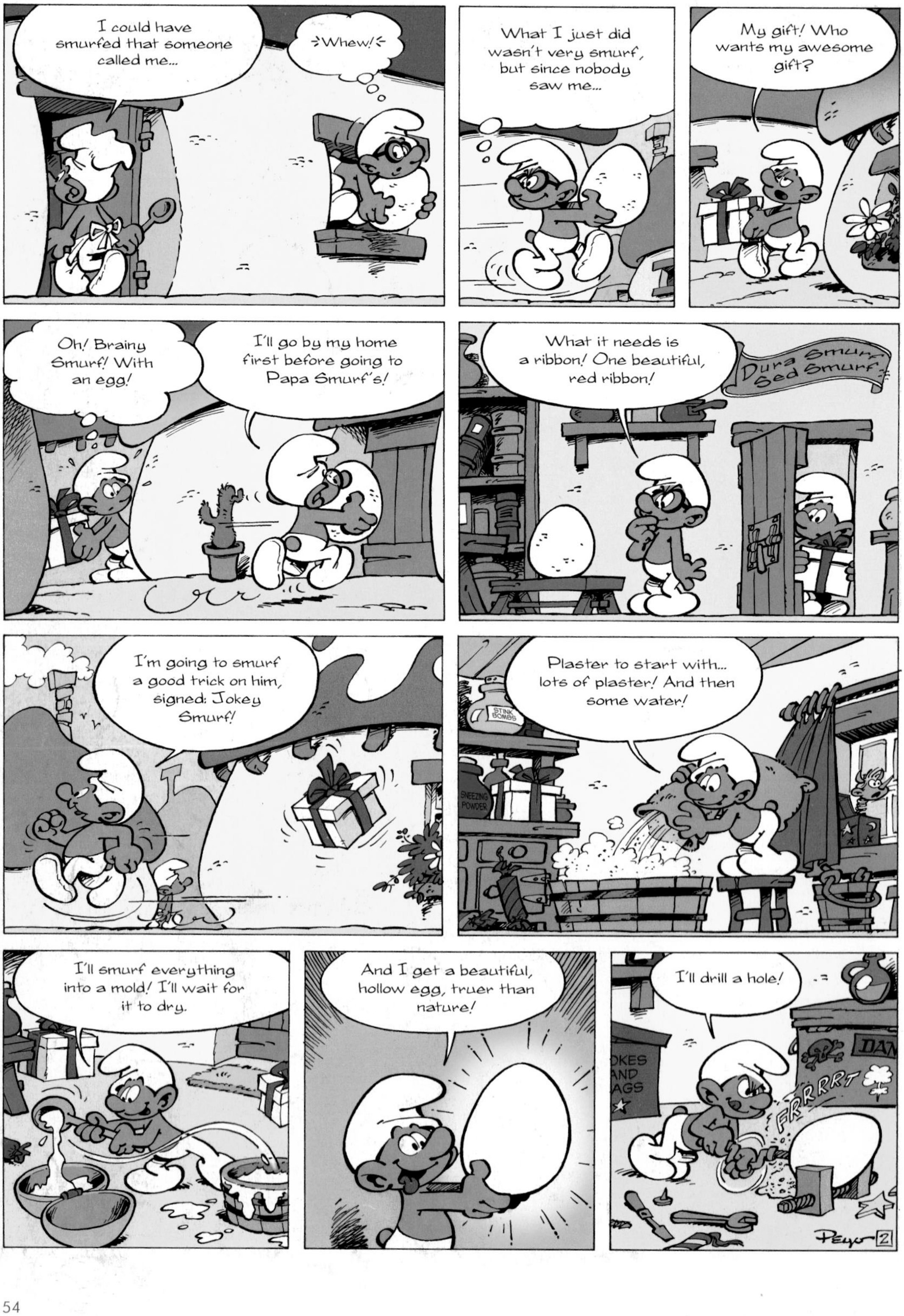
I could have smurfed that someone called me...
Whew!
What I just did wasn't very smurf, but since nobody saw me...
My gift! Who wants my awesome gift?
Oh! Brainy Smurf! With an egg!
I'll go by my home first before going to Papa Smurf's!
What it needs is a ribbon! One beautiful, red ribbon!
Dura Smurf Sed Smurf
I'm going to smurf a good trick on him, signed: Jokey Smurf!
Plaster to start with... lots of plaster! And then some water!
STINK BOMBS
SNEEZING POWDER
I'll smurf everything into a mold! I'll wait for it to dry.
And I get a beautiful, hollow egg, truer than nature!
I'll drill a hole!
FRRRRRT
Peyo
2

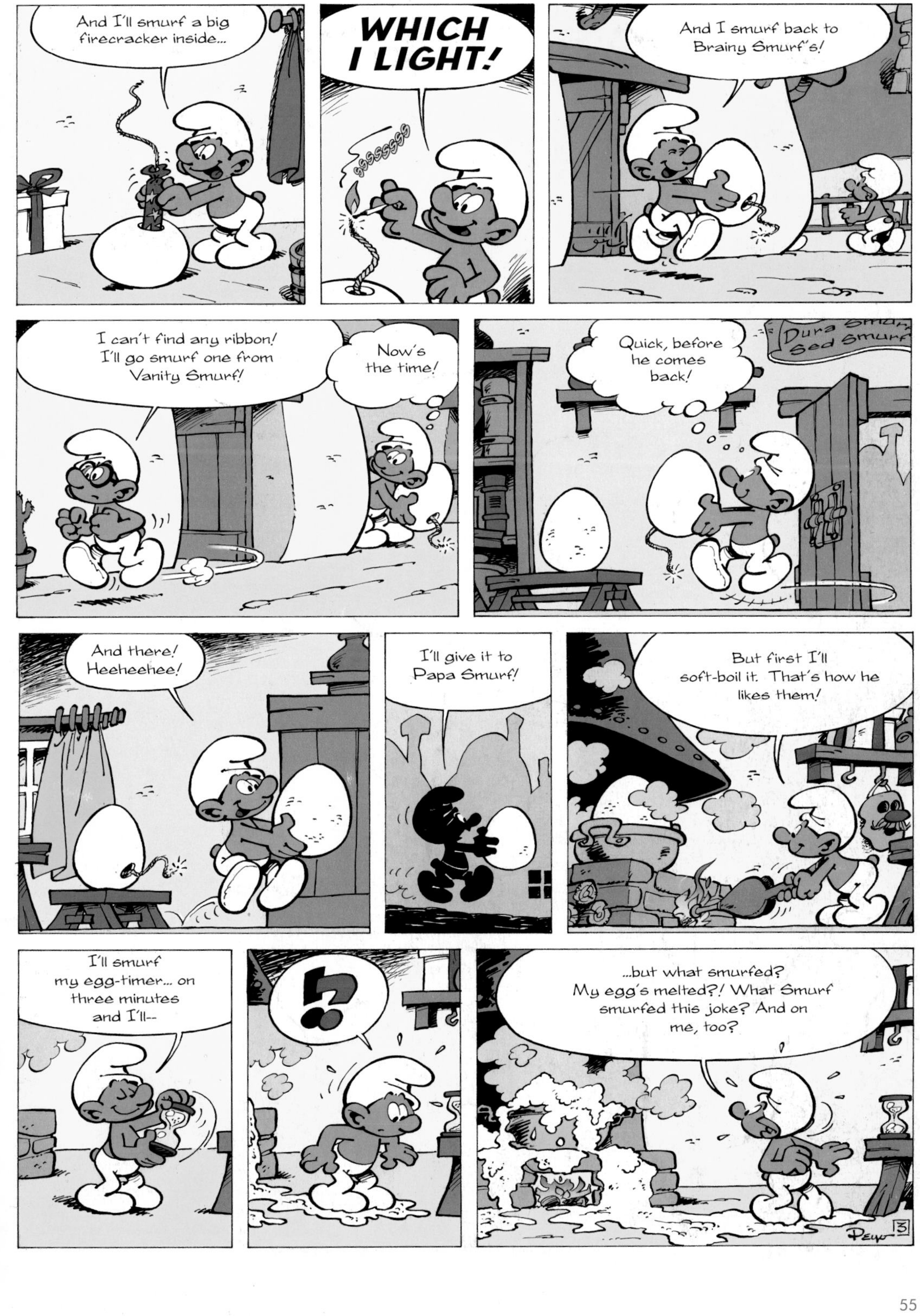
And I'll smurf a big firecracker inside...
WHICH I LIGHT!
SSSSSSSS
And I smurf back to Brainy Smurf's!
I can't find any ribbon! I'll go smurf one from Vanity Smurf!
Now's the time!
Quick, before he comes back!
And there! Heeheehee!
I'll give it to Papa Smurf!
But first I'll soft-boil it. That's how he likes them!
I'll smurf my egg-timer... on three minutes and I'll--
!?
...but what smurfed? My egg's melted?! What Smurf smurfed this joke? And on me, too?
Peyo
13

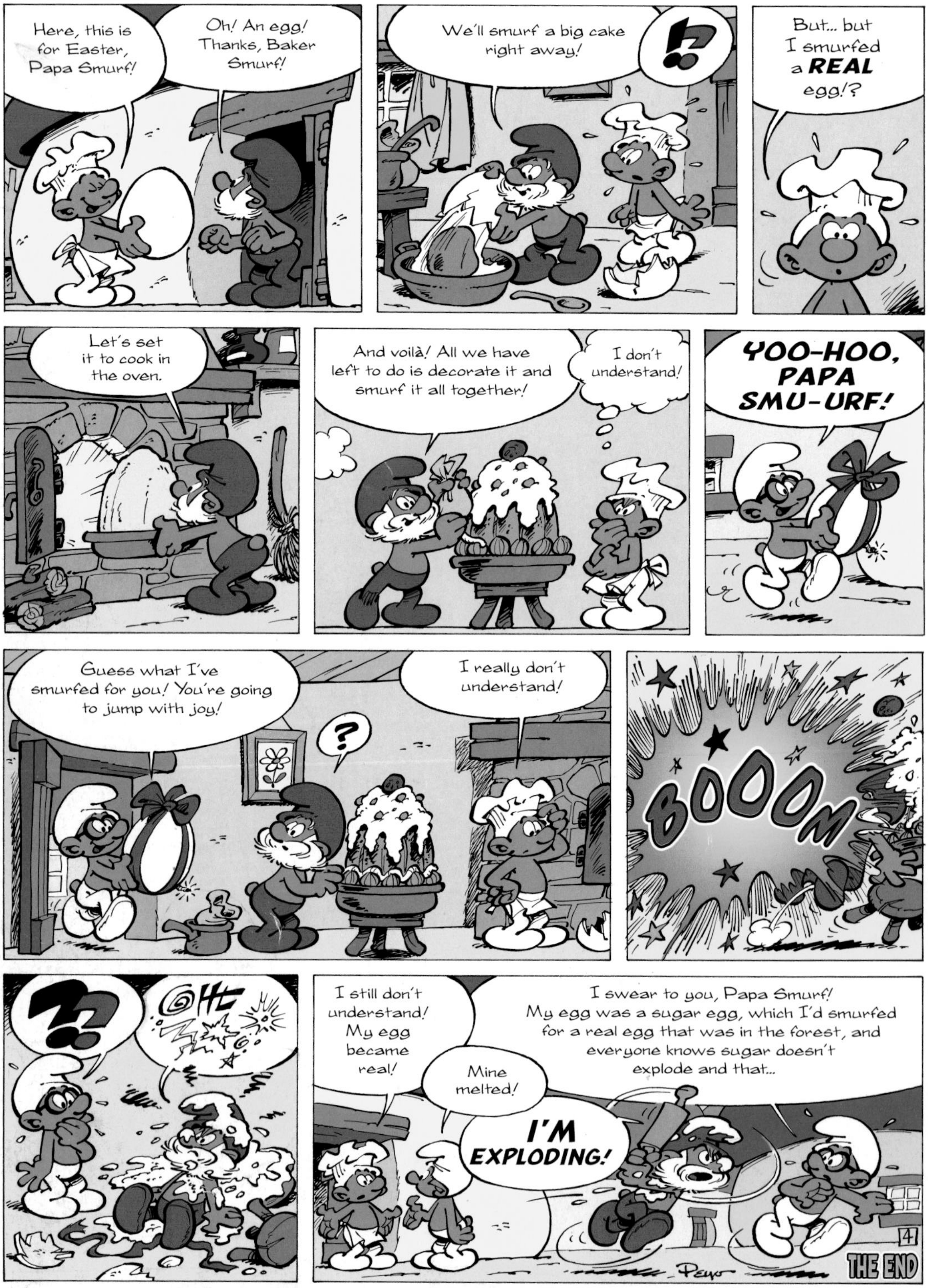

Here, this is for Easter, Papa Smurf!
Oh! An egg! Thanks, Baker Smurf!
We'll smurf a big cake right away!
!?
But... but I smurfed a **REAL** egg!?
Let's set it to cook in the oven.
And voilà! All we have left to do is decorate it and smurf it all together!
I don't understand!
YOO-HOO, PAPA SMU-URF!
Guess what I've smurfed for you! You're going to jump with joy!
?
I really don't understand!
BOOOM
??
I still don't understand! My egg became real!
Mine melted!
I'M EXPLODING!
I swear to you, Papa Smurf! My egg was a sugar egg, which I'd smurfed for a real egg that was in the forest, and everyone knows sugar doesn't explode and that...
4
THE END

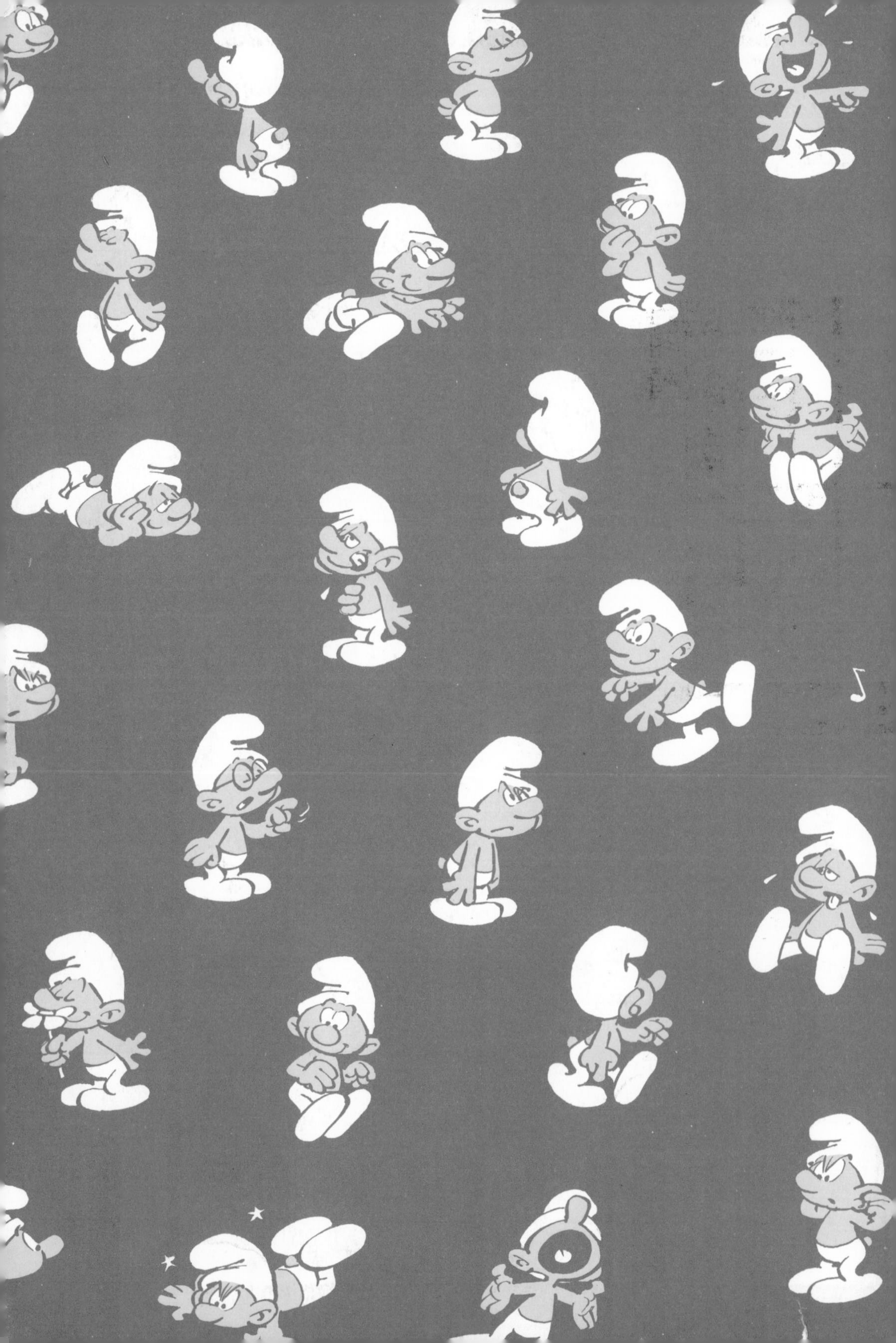